A horn blast tore through the air.

Sam snapped his head around. His feet became jelly. He hadn't looked before he'd rushed into the street. He heard the tires screeching and perceived only a massive blur, framed by the dark gray drabness of the winter landscape. He knew it was a car, though, and that it was going too fast to stop in time. In seeming slow motion the blur consumed his entire field of vision . . . drowning out all other sights and sounds until there was nothing.

He was about to ask himself a question, but he never had the chance.

Don't miss any books in this thrilling series:

FEARLESS™

Available from POCKET PULSE

FEARLESS™

LIAR

FRANCINE PASCAL

POCKET PULSE
New York   London   Toronto   Sydney   Singapore

To Taryn Adler

An *Original* Publication *of* POCKET BOOKS

POCKET PULSE, published by
Pocket Books, a division of Simon & Schuster, Inc.
1230 Avenue of the Americas, New York, NY 10020

Produced by 17th Street Productions,
an Alloy Online, Inc. company
33 West 17th Street
New York, NY 10011

Copyright © 2000 by Francine Pascal

Cover art copyright © 2000 by 17th Street Productions,
an Alloy Online, Inc. company.
Cover photography by St. Denis. Cover design by Mike Rivilis.

ISBN: 0-671-03951-2

First Pocket Pulse Paperback printing July 2000

10 9 8 7 6 5 4 3 2

Fearless™ is a trademark of Francine Pascal.
POCKET PULSE and colophon are
trademarks of Simon & Schuster, Inc.

Printed in the U.S.A.

I read somewhere once that there
are four stages of grief. Or
maybe five. I can't remember.
Which is kind of strange because
I have a great memory.
Photographic, in fact. All the
shitty things that have ever happened to me are permanently
burned into my mind, like a continuous movie. And it's not a
movie you would want to pay eight
bucks for, either—no heroes or
happy endings, just a lot of sadness and destruction.

Anyway, the first stage is
denial. That's one I can understand. In fact, it's probably the
reason why I don't remember the
stages of grief in the first
place—because for a while there,
I didn't want to believe that
grief even existed. If I can't
feel fear, then why should I feel
grief? I mean, it makes sense,
right? I don't even have to deny
fear. It just doesn't exist.
Things are much easier to deal
with if they don't exist.

The next stage is anger. (I think.) That's also another one that makes perfect sense to me. For example, when I finally realized that my friend Mary Moss was truly *gone*, that she was never coming back, *ever*—I got pissed.

So I went on a little mission. I decided to murder somebody.

That somebody was Skizz, the asshole coke dealer who ended Mary's life. Luckily, another somebody beat me to it. *Barely.* Skizz died in front of my eyes.

Even more luckily, I was reborn.

I know that sounds really lame and cheesy, but it's true. I realized that by going on this mission—by thinking of nothing else except murdering a scumbag whose life isn't worth the coke he sells—I was losing the one person I have left. Ed Fargo.

This isn't an exaggeration, by the way. I'm not being melodramatic. Ed *is* the only person I have left in the world.

I know what you're thinking. Don't I have *anyone*?

What about my mom, for instance? Nope. Gone.

My dad? Also gone. Missing in action the night Mom died.

George, my guardian of the moment? Nice, sweet, sincere—but not really there for me.

Ella, the evil bitch who happens to be George's coguardian? Best not to go there.

Which brings me to Sam. Sam Moon, the guy who haunts me, the guy I obsess over; the boy goes out with Heather Gannis. . . . Okay, it's best not to go *there*, either. But for a brief moment I thought Sam and I had made a breakthrough. That is, until he showed up at my door, took one look at the Wicked Witch of the West Village (Ella, in case you haven't guessed), then bolted. Not that I can blame him for running away from *her*. Still, it was kind of weird. And I've only

seen him once since. I basically
told him to screw off.

Of course, that was when I was
still in the "anger" stage.

I'm pretty sure the last stage
of grief is acceptance. Which is
where I am now. I accept that
Mary's dead. I accept that Sam
Moon and I will never happen. I
accept that my life sucks, that
danger stalks me like a psychotic
villain, that I'll live the rest
of my life with no friends except
a guy without feeling in his
legs.

I guess that means I'm fully
recovered, right?

A little
Charles
Manson
and a
little
Mother
Teresa . . . .

gaia's problem

GAIA STARED BLANKLY AT THE book on her desk. She almost laughed. What was she thinking? Did she really believe she would spend Friday evening in this lame little bedroom and actually *read*? Maybe

The Beauty of Ed

she was finally pulling herself together after the trauma of Mary's death—but still, normalcy came in stages. It came in baby steps. And reading *The Great Gatsby* in the Nivens' house felt like a giant step clear into somebody else's life.

Besides, nobody did homework on Fridays. Not even the ultranormal. Not even studious people like . . . well, like Sam Moon. Not even if *The Great Gatsby* was the great work of literature everyone said it was.

Time to bolt. Bolting was a specialty of hers.

Gaia sighed and brushed a few tangled strands of blond hair out of her face, then pushed herself away from the desk. Part of the problem was that Ella was home, and even though Gaia had avoided her (Ella was locked in her bedroom, listening to some horrid Celine Dion CD), the knowledge that they were under the same roof was enough to make Gaia want to puke.

She stood up and stretched, peering out the window. It was cold and dark—but that had never stopped her from going out before. Maybe she'd go to the park and try to hustle a chess game. Or maybe she'd swing by Ed's and see if he wanted to see a movie. She grinned. That sounded perfect, actually. Ed would definitely be up for something. He hated being stuck in his bedroom almost as much as Gaia hated—

"I'm sorry about your friend."

What the hell?

Gaia whirled around, her blue eyes smoldering.

Ella was standing in the open doorway—decked out, as usual, as if she were going to model at a teen fashion show. Today's outfit consisted of a tight baby T-shirt that wouldn't fit a dwarf, black leather mini-skirt, and boots. And her red hair was in pigtails. Freaking pigtails. It was almost funny.

"Don't you knock?" Gaia asked.

Ella stared back at her blankly. "Not in my own house," she replied.

Touché, Gaia thought. That was classic Ella. Always reminding Gaia of her place. Always making sure Gaia knew who was in charge. And this was Ella's house. Not Gaia's. It never would be. At least that was something they could agree on.

"So what do you want?" Gaia demanded impatiently, turning toward her closet.

"I just wanted to tell you that I'm sorry about your friend," Ella repeated. Her tone was colorless, without emotion. "You know. The one who died."

Gaia froze. She scowled. *Sorry about your friend?* Please. Ella didn't give a shit about anyone but herself. And she sure as hell had never offered any kind of sympathy toward Gaia before.

"What do you really want, Ella?" Gaia asked, looking her directly in the eye.

"I told you," Ella replied.

"You're . . . sorry," Gaia stated dubiously.

Ella's face darkened. "Look, just forget it. I . . ." She bit her lip, hesitating. Finally she shook her head. "Forget it," she said again. "This isn't going to work." She turned and strode down the steps.

A moment later Ella's bedroom door slammed.

Gaia's jaw fell open. In all the months she'd been stuck in this freakish house, that was by far the most bizarre encounter she'd ever had. And disquieting, too—much more so than any of their arguments. That's because their arguments made sense. Even when Gaia had smacked Ella in the face a couple of months ago, there had been some kind of logic involved. Ella had said something particularly loathsome. Therefore Gaia had found herself throwing a punch. *A* led to *B,* which led to *C.* Gaia had regretted hitting her; she'd promised it would never happen again—but Ella had provoked the incident. It hadn't come out of *nowhere.*

Not like this.

So. That posed a very disturbing question.

Could it be that Ella actually *meant* what she said? That she was sorry about Mary?

No. Gaia shook her head. Of course not. This was the woman who treated Gaia like dirt . . . who was using her unsuspecting husband for some sinister purpose Gaia had yet to determine—but that probably involved embezzlement and sleazy affairs with one or more men. Ella was evil. Plain and simple. This was just another manifestation of Ella's multiple personality disorder: slipping from mask to mask without ever revealing her true face.

Still, what had she meant by *"This isn't going to work"*? It sounded like the kind of thing that somebody would say if they were trying to mend a relationship. But she and Ella didn't have a relationship of any kind. At all.

Gaia took a deep breath. She took two quick steps across her room and picked up the phone, then punched in Ed's number.

After two rings he picked up. "Hello?"

Ed's voice could always make Gaia smile. It was so open, so friendly—but with an edge, too.

"Hey, Ed," she whispered.

"Hey, I think we've got a psychic connection," Ed remarked dryly.

"Why's that?"

"Because I was just about to call *you*. My new wheelchair came today while we were at school. I wanted to show it off. It's radical. I'm talking state-of-the-art. Power steering. It goes from zero to sixty in four hours. Faster down a flight of subway steps, of course."

Gaia wanted to give Ed credit for being funny, but she couldn't muster a laugh. "Sounds good," she mumbled. "Actually I was . . . um, I was just calling to see if you wanted to go see a movie. Or rent one, maybe."

"Sure." There was a pause. "Are you okay?"

"Yeah," she said automatically. But then she frowned. In the past she would have shrugged off Ed's questions or told him to mind his own business. But after the events of the past week—after she'd nearly killed Ed and destroyed his wheelchair on the afore-mentioned subway steps—she was determined not to hide from him anymore. He was her one friend, so she might as well treat him like one.

"Nothing's wrong?" Ed prodded.

She flopped down on her bed, twirling the phone cord in her fingers. It took a few seconds to get the words out. "Actually, there *is* something wrong."

"What's that?" Ed's voice registered both surprise and happiness. Not that there was something wrong, but that Gaia was telling him so.

"Ella."

"Something new?" Ed asked.

"She told me she's sorry about Mary."

Ed was silent. "And that is bad because . . . ?"

"Come on, Ed. I would have felt better if she'd punched me in the face. I'm comfortable with our mutual hatred. Her pretending to care really gave me the creeps."

Ed fell silent again.

"Hello? Ed?"

"Maybe she *is* sorry," he suggested.

Gaia rolled her eyes. "Believe me, she isn't. The woman is completely evil."

"Mmmm," he said equivocally.

"What, mmmm?" Gaia asked, frowning. If she was going to be open and honest, the least Ed could do was agree with everything she said.

"Listen to me, Gaia," Ed said. "Nobody's completely evil."

"Oh, no?" she asked, raising her eyebrows. "Why's that?"

"Well, I guess there's Charles Manson. But ninety-nine-point-nine percent of people aren't completely anything. See, it's like . . . you've got Charles Manson on one side of the spectrum and Mother Teresa on the other. The rest of us are in between. Aside from a very few extremes, nobody's *all* good or *all* bad."

"I didn't know you were such a philosopher, Ed."

"Being in a wheelchair makes a person philosophical," he replied. His tone wasn't self-pitying; it was matter-of-fact. That was one of the things Gaia loved about Ed most: He never let people feel sorry for him because of his accident. He took people's pity and threw it right back in their teeth.

"So you're saying that everybody's got a little Manson and a little Mother Teresa inside them?" Gaia asked.

"Exactly," Ed stated confidently.

"I'd say Ella's snuggled up pretty close to Charles Manson," Gaia theorized.

"Maybe Ella is mostly Manson," he agreed. "But today she let her pinprick of Mother Teresa shine through."

Yeah, right. As much as Gaia wanted to tell Ed that he was full of crap, she laughed instead. That was the beauty of Ed. He could take any asinine theory and improve a person's mood with it.

"So are we gonna rent a movie or what?" Gaia asked cheerfully.

"Sure. Meet me at the Blockbuster by Thirteenth and Broadway."

"Yup."

"And maybe after that we can go to Alice Underground and buy me a blazer."

"Why would we want to do that?" Gaia asked.

"Because I need to wear a jacket and tie to an engagement party."

Gaia picked at her thumbnail. "Who's getting engaged?"

"My sister. She's marrying a guy named Blane."

Gaia sat up on the bed. "Your sister? Really?" she asked, genuinely surprised. Ed hardly ever talked about his sister. Gaia got the feeling the mysterious other Fargo sibling didn't take many opportunities to hang around Ed.

"Yeah. Blane."

"Weird."

"Yeah, so I'll see you at Blockbuster in twenty minutes," Ed said.

"You got it." Gaia hung up the phone. She sat on her bed for a few seconds, staring into space.

Amazing. She couldn't even remember why Ella had freaked her out so much. Maybe Ella *was* letting her Mother Teresa shine through.

Sure. And maybe Gaia would end up marrying a guy named Blane, too. It was great to be back in the denial stage again.

Two to Tango

SAM MOON EXHALED DEEPLY, WATCHING his breath billow in the frigid January air. He'd been freezing his ass off in the alley by Gaia's brownstone for almost half an hour, and his toes were beginning to burn. He stomped his boots on the pavement to get the circulation going. But all *that* did was rattle his bones—

"Whoa!"

His legs went out from under him. All of a sudden he was slipping wildly out of control. His overcoat flapped like a cape. His arms flailed. He lunged for a nearby railing to steady himself, just barely keeping balance, and hoisted himself to his feet.

A scowl crossed his face.

Jesus. His lungs heaved. He ran his frozen fingers through his tousled hair and shook his head, then glanced down at the ground. He couldn't even see any ice—just a layer of glistening blackness over the concrete slabs of the sidewalk. Great. Even the *sidewalk* seemed to be laying a trap for him.

Traps. He shook his head and glanced up at Gaia's front door. He knew all about them. All about deception. Oh, yes. A sickening queasiness began to gnaw at his insides. The last time he'd opened that door, he'd felt like he'd walked into the biggest trap of his life. . . .

"No," he whispered out loud.

That image was so clearly etched into his mind: the image of Gaia's foster mother, standing just inside the doorway, smiling seductively at him over Gaia's shoulder. Just *thinking* about her made him want to vomit. He couldn't believe he'd allowed himself to be seduced by her. He couldn't believe she would *want* to seduce him. He couldn't believe she'd continued to hound him with e-mails and calls and all the rest of it. . . .

But the most nauseating part was that the blame didn't fall solely on her. No. He was to blame, too. After all, their sordid encounter fit the stupid cliché, didn't it? *It takes two to tango.* He'd slept with Ella willingly. He'd allowed her to sweet-talk him at that bar, to dance . . . to take his mind and body to some other place. Of course, at the time he'd had no idea that she was Gaia's legal guardian—but still, he'd consciously cheated on his girlfriend. His beautiful, unsuspecting girlfriend. The one he should love but couldn't.

For a moment Sam's mind changed gears. That very beautiful unsuspecting girlfriend may or may not have cheated on him. That was partly why he'd been at the bar in the first place. *Bullshit*, he growled at himself impatiently. Heather wasn't the cause of his torment. Gaia was. Gaia always was.

His jaw tightened. Now he had to confront Ella. He had to make sure she left him alone, that she stopped hassling him—and most of all, that she never, *ever* told Gaia what had happened.

Out of the corner of his eye Sam caught a glimpse of an NYPD cruiser, rounding the corner and turning onto Perry Street. It slowed as it rumbled past him. Two craggy, tough-looking members of New York's finest gave him a once-over. Sam averted his eyes. Maybe they thought he was a stalker. He almost laughed. He *did* look a little sketchy—disheveled after his near fall. But suspecting him would be pretty ironic, wouldn't it? He was here to *stop* a stalker: the woman who was harassing him with e-mails and phone calls. He was here to insist that she stop, to issue his own version of . . . what was it called? A restraining order. That was it. He was going to demand that Ella leave him alone. Forever.

Yes. For once in his life Sam Moon was going to set everything straight. He took a deep breath and turned his attention back to the closed door. He was tired of waffling and wavering, of dating Heather but desiring Gaia, of acting out his anger and frustration by behaving in ways he only regretted. It was time to make some decisions. To go after what he wanted. To follow his heart—

His heart nearly stopped as the front door swung open. He sucked in his breath.

It wasn't Ella. It was Gaia. She bounded down the steps . . . right past him, without even so much as a glance in his direction.

Gaia!

He wanted to shout her name. But he couldn't. He'd been robbed of speech. He stood there, paralyzed—unable to move, unable to breathe, unable to do anything but watch as she trotted down the street, her blond mane streaming from under her ratty black wool hat. Even from behind, she was like some kind of . . . well, *vision*—not like any other girl he'd ever seen or known.

Every time he laid eyes on her, he was entranced by that intangible quality that separated her from everyone else—the way she carried herself that he could never quite place. It wasn't just that she was beautiful: tall and strong, like those mythical women of the Amazon. It was more that she had no *idea* she was beautiful.

Generally speaking, girls in Manhattan tended to know they were hot. They strutted around in the latest trends, self-possessed and perfectly put together . . . like Heather, in a way. Or Ella. Not Gaia, though. Gaia—

The front door opened again.

Without thinking, Sam ducked behind the railing.

It was Ella, of course. Sam shook his head, furious at himself. He was here to *confront* her! So why the hell was he crouched down, hiding from her in the freezing cold like a frightened animal? Actually, he didn't want to answer that question.

TOM MOORE SAT PERFECTLY RIGID AS

An Expert Gaia strolled past his parked brown Lexus. If she turned her head only the slightest bit, she might see him. He silently swore under his breath. He knew he shouldn't have driven here. And he shouldn't have parked so close to the Nivens' house. But he'd had no choice. This was the only spot available in an eight-block radius. In New York City parking spaces were like taxicabs: They were impossible to find when you needed one. Besides, the car was equipped with certain devices essential for today's mission—a satellite link and fax machine—that he couldn't carry on his person.

Don't look at me, Gaia. Don't look. . . .

He slouched down low in the driver's seat, staring at her.

Every day she looked more and more like her mother.

A lump formed in Tom's throat. He shook his head. Here he was, not ten feet away from his daughter, and he still couldn't touch her. He couldn't call her name. But that was nothing new. He'd learned to live with frustration. That was part of the job. He was a professional. Not a day went by when an agent didn't suffer in some way. But the best of them compartmentalized the suffering—locking it safely away with the rest of their souls, where it couldn't affect other matters.

Tom was an expert at compartmentalizing.

Gaia crossed to the opposite corner. Tom couldn't help but notice that her walk was like a taller, lankier version of Katia's—strong and sensual at the same time. . . .

His eyes flashed back to the house. Ella was leaving. George would be home in a matter of minutes.

But maybe he could follow Gaia for a little while, just to make sure she was okay. Yes. There was no telling when Loki would strike—

What am I thinking?

Following her would be inconceivably stupid. For one thing, he'd lose his parking space. For another, Gaia might notice him. No, she *would* notice him. She'd been trained to detect tails; he himself had conducted the relentless drills, day after day in their old home in their old life . . . so long ago.

But George's words from their last meeting kept echoing through his head. They blasted away at his common sense, reducing it to rubble. *"Loki's interest in our girl has taken on a new twist. There's reason to believe he wants her—for himself."*

Tom shook his head. Screw common sense. No way would he let Gaia out of his sight. He grabbed the key out of his pocket and jammed it into the ignition.

The Dead Girl

ELLA PAUSED ON THE SIDEWALK. SHE was fumbling for something in the pocket of her faux fur coat . . . a cell phone. She flipped it open and began walking briskly in the opposite direction Gaia had headed, away from Washington Square Park.

". . . doesn't need to be monitored every second," she was saying.

At least that's what Sam *thought* she was saying. Her voice trailed off, lost in the ambient noise of the city.

He hesitated. This was stupid. Even worse, it was shameful. He was *going* to confront her. Summoning his courage, he stood up straight and marched purposefully after her.

Ella suddenly stopped in midstep.

"The dead girl's not an issue anymore," she stated. "Gaia's problem was solved. *You* solved it."

Sam's pace slowed . . . then he stopped altogether. At the mention of Gaia's name, he found he couldn't continue. His face twisted in a scowl. *The dead girl? Gaia's problem?* He shook his head. Could it be that Ella was talking about Mary? No. No way. Mary wasn't Gaia's *problem.* On the other hand . . . what could she possibly mean?

Ella snapped the cell phone shut and scurried across the street.

Sam swallowed. *Follow her, dammit!* He clenched his fists at his sides and darted after her, splashing into a puddle of brownish slush as he leaped off the curb.

GAIA PAUSED ON THE OPPOSITE CORNER,

Shadowy

struck by the sound of an engine. She'd noticed it a few seconds ago—loud at first, which meant that the driver was in a hurry, then very soft. Which meant that the driver was being cautious.

Or following someone.

The chances that the driver was following *her* were probably small. Still, it was good to have a `healthy paranoia`. She turned and peered through the early evening twilight at a brown car, idling on the opposite curb. Her eyes narrowed. The driver was a man. . . . She couldn't make out any of his features, just a shadowy silhouette.

Instinctively she stepped forward. The car suddenly jumped to life, pulling out into the street. Shit. But then her eyes zeroed in on something else.

No, *somebody* else.

What the—

A HORN BLAST TORE THROUGH THE AIR.

Unanswered Question

Sam snapped his head around. His feet became jelly. He hadn't looked before he'd rushed into the street. He heard the tires screeching and perceived only a massive blur, framed by the dark gray drabness of the winter landscape. He knew it was a car, though, and that it was going too fast to stop in time. In seeming slow motion the blur consumed his entire field of vision ... drowning out all other sights and sounds until there was nothing.

He was about to ask himself a question, but he never had the chance.

"JESUS CHRIST!"

Tom Moore furiously stamped the brake, but the pavement was too slick. *No, no, no.* The car wouldn't stop. It was careening out of control. That kid, that *idiot* kid—why had he run out into the middle of the street? The tires whined. Tom cringed involuntarily. But at the moment of impact he was struck by two simultaneous realizations: one, that he *recognized* the kid; two, that Gaia was flinging herself in front of the car and shoving the kid to safety.

"No!"

The word erupted from Tom's mouth the instant the hood struck his daughter. Flesh and metal connected with a sickening thud. Tom watched dumbstruck as Gaia's body hurtled up into the air and then slammed into the windshield. He threw his hands in front of his face. But miraculously the car lurched to a stop.

Gaia rolled onto the pavement, disappearing from his view.

Silence.

Time came to an instant standstill. The world ceased to turn. Tom didn't hear a sound. He couldn't breathe. His mind shut down but for one horrible thought.

I've just killed my own daughter.

But then something else crept into his consciousness . . . a noise. Shouting. The kid. He was back in the street, grabbing Gaia and propping up her head. Tom could just barely see her over the hood. His heart rattled like a machine gun. His body felt like it was on fire.

What have I done? What have I—

And then he saw it. Yes! Oh God, she was alive. A warm rush of relief seeped through his veins as he saw the wisp of frozen vapor drift up from under his daughter's nose. She was breathing. She was alive. Thank God she knew how to relax during a collision, to let the force of impact throw her body as if she were a sack of potatoes. One of the first lessons of martial arts was minimizing injury. She would be bruised, maybe even have a few cracked bones . . . but she would survive.

He gazed at her transfixed, watching in blessed

relief as Gaia lifted her head and blinked her eyelids, pulling the world into focus. He read the single word on her lips:

"Shit."

He let his breath go. That was his Gaia.

He shoved his panic aside and thrust the car into reverse, simultaneously reaching for the car phone. As the car jumped backward, he punched in three numbers: 911.

"Emergency," a voice answered.

"I'd like to report a hit and run at the corner of West Fourth and Perry Street," Tom hissed. "You better call an ambulance."

He pulled the car around the corner. He'd abandon the car just west of Bleecker and return to the scene of the accident to make certain Gaia was all right. It wasn't a hit and run exactly. More of a hit and hide.

AT FIRST THE SEQUENCE OF EVENTS didn't register in Sam's brain. Everything seemed to swirl together like some nightmarish impressionist painting. One moment he was about to get hit by a car; the next he was lying

The Horror

on the sidewalk, staring at Gaia as she lay in a heap on the street. And now he was holding her. Cradling her in his arms. Praying that she was alive, that the bastard who'd hit her hadn't killed her . . .

"Come on, Gaia," he heard himself whisper. But the words seemed to come from some other place—as if he were standing off to the side, watching the horror as it unfolded. "Come on—"

She moaned. A flicker of hope sparked inside him. He pushed tangled hair away from her lovely face. "Gaia, please be okay," he whispered. She had a cut along her cheekbone. He held her closer, bending so close to her, his lips nearly touched her forehead. "Please," he whispered again.

Suddenly he felt her body stiffen. Slowly, mercifully, she lifted her head and opened her eyes. Oh, Christ, she was going to be okay. His heart seemed to levitate above his chest.

"Shit," she muttered, curling her body in pain.

Sam's head snapped up at the noisy strain of a car engine backing up in a hurry. Before he could clear his head, the car had disappeared around the corner, speeding crazily in reverse down West Fourth Street. Dammit. He wished he'd had the sense to get the bastard's license plate number. What kind of shameless asshole would hit an innocent girl and speed away?

Plenty of people in New York City, Sam answered

25

his own question. People ran over each other every single goddamn day. And nobody cared. Nobody wanted to get involved. Nobody wanted to take responsibility.

He urgently scanned the street for Ella, for an onlooker, for *anyone*. Gaia needed an ambulance. But the sidewalks were deserted.

"Sam?" Gaia whispered.

He gazed down at her, startled. A drop of blood trickled over the ledge of her chin onto the sleeve of his coat.

"I'm here," he murmured. "Just hold on. . . ."

Sirens were approaching. He could hear the distant wail, drawing closer and closer.

"Sam?" Gaia repeated. She squirmed in his arms.

He hugged her as tightly as he could. "Shhh," he whispered. "They'll be here—"

"Do you think you could let go of me?" she finally managed.

His eyes widened. She squirmed harder.

"But I—I—just . . . I didn't," he started stammering incoherently.

"I'm *fine*," she grunted. Her eyes were open now— alert, awake, fixed on him with a cold intensity. "Just let me go."

The sirens grew louder.

Let you go? Sam stared at her, slack jawed. Didn't she know that she'd almost been killed? His grip on

26

her loosened—and in that instant Gaia pushed herself away and staggered back toward her house.

"Gaia!" he shouted. "Gaia, please don't go—I need to—Gaia!"

But if she heard him, she didn't show it. She stumbled up the stoop and through the door and slammed it behind her, leaving Sam alone on the frozen pavement.

The street was eerily silent. "I need to thank you," he finished to nobody at all. "Thank you for saving my life."

So my wildest fantasy finally came true. Yup. The impossible happened. I told Gaia Moore that I loved her. And she told me that she loved me. I mean, this is the moment I've been dreaming of non-stop for four months.

I don't even think I can explain it. Imagine this: You know the very first guy who ever walked on the moon? Neil Armstrong? I'm pretty sure that's his name. Anyway, pic- ture him as a little boy, look- ing up at the night sky (and remember, this was probably back in the thirties, when air- planes were still brand-new) and telling his mom: "Mommy, I'm gonna fly to the moon some- day." She probably laughed and patted him on the back and thought: *Little boys can be so stupid sometimes.*

And then—a mere thirty years later—he does it. Ha! Bite me, Mom!

Well, for the record: Having

Gaia Moore tell you that she
loves you is way more impressive
than flying to the moon.

Right. Of course, the fact
that Gaia Moore made this confession to me doesn't mean squat.
Oh, yeah. Did I forget to mention
that there was a shitty element
to the whole equation?

See, I *always* knew that she
loved me—on a certain level. As
a friend. A best friend, even.
Just not in . . . "that way."
She never will, either. When she
hugged me on the subway steps
after nearly killing me and when
she made that speech at Mary's
funeral, we reached a new understanding. We can share things
now. We can afford to be vulnerable around each other. I know
all of this sounds like I ripped
it off from some made-for-TV
movie on the Lifetime channel,
but it's true. It's a whole new
level.

The flip side is that this
whole new level makes it

painfully clear that we're never
going to be involved in . . .
"that way."

Don't get me wrong. The new
level is great. Maybe I'll
finally find out what those deep,
dark secrets of hers *are*, anyway.
Which would be awesome. Amazing.
Radical, as I used to say—when my
legs worked and I went by the
name of Shred and kicked serious
butt on a skateboard.

But even if she does bare her
soul, she still won't think of me
in . . . "that way." In fact, the
more she does confide in me, the
less likely she'll ever be
attracted to me. Generally speaking, people don't date their best
friends.

Which kind of sucks.

Her flesh
burned; her
body ached—**sexual**
but the
frustration
agony was
tolerable.

ED FARGO WHEELED BACK AND FORTH

down the aisles of the Village Blockbuster: his version of pacing. He was starting to get impatient. Scratch that. He was starting to get seriously annoyed. Gaia was supposed to meet him—when? Forty-seven minutes ago?

The Gaia Effect

She'd probably gotten held up by Ella. Or maybe she'd decided to stop in the park for a quick game of ice-cold, subzero chess on her way up to meet him. No, what probably happened was this: She'd decided to pick a fight with a gang of demented serial killers and ended up getting blown away with a machine gun— but not before kicking eight guys' asses at once.

Ed smiled queasily as he passed the long row of new releases. That wasn't very funny, actually. Something like that *could* happen to Gaia. Something like that happened to Gaia almost every freaking week.

Okay. There was no point in speculating. He'd give her a few more minutes, and then he'd call her. Right. In the meantime he'd pick a movie for them. His eyes roved over some big-budget comedy starring Mike Myers (nah) . . . then to the tearjerkers (would Gaia submit to a chick flick?) . . . after that the Tom Hanks vehicles (that guy probably counted as a genre unto himself by now) . . . but he was unable to focus on anything. There was no way he could pick a movie.

The thing was, he didn't even really *want* to watch a movie. The movie was just an excuse. What he really wanted to do was ask Gaia if she wanted to come to his sister's stupid engagement party with him.

It wouldn't be a date, of course. Not technically. Ed just wanted some company, somebody to s h a r e i n h i s m i s e r y. On the other hand, it *would* provide a convenient excuse to see Gaia in some sexy formal wear—

Wait a second.

He knew *exactly* what to rent. Duh. *The Great Gatsby.* It sure as hell beat reading the book. And his mom had mentioned that they made a movie of it a long time ago, starring Robert Redford. She'd even said it was good. If he provided Gaia with an alternative to doing her homework, then she'd owe him. She'd *have* to go to the party with him.

He deftly maneuvered his way through the Friday night rental crowd and wheeled up to the information counter. A pimply, bored-looking girl in a blue uniform was standing behind it, chewing gum.

"Excuse me?" he asked. "Do you know if *The Great Gatsby* is in?"

She nodded. "Yeah. It isn't."

Ed frowned. "It isn't?"

The girl blew a bubble. It popped with a sticky smack. She sucked the goo back into her mouth and pointed at somebody. "Nope. That girl over there just checked it out."

Ed followed her outstretched finger—and rolled his eyes.

"That girl" was none other than his lovely ex-girlfriend, Heather Gannis. She was standing in line at the checkout counter, smiling impishly and waving the movie at him. He smiled. He should have figured this would happen. After all, Heather was the master at blowing off work by substituting movies for books. Back when they were going out, the two of them had stayed up all night watching a Shakespeare movie marathon in preparation for their English finals: *Hamlet* with Mel Gibson, *Romeo and Juliet* with Leonardo DiCaprio. One thing about Heather: She was very reliable—at least when it came to being dishonest. He wondered if she'd ever done any *legitimate* studying.

She waltzed over to him and dropped the video box into his lap.

"So, Shred, you wouldn't happen to be looking for an easy way out of reading *The Great Gatsby*, would you?" she teased.

He gazed back at her with a perfectly straight face. "Actually, I just wanted to compare the film and literary versions for my own edification."

She smirked. "Right. Me too."

"What can I say, Heather?" He bowed his head and shook it. "You beat me."

36

"Well, why don't you just come over and watch it with me?" she asked.

He blinked. "Excuse me?"

She shrugged. "Why not? I mean, we both have to see it, right? Either that or you go home and spend all weekend reading the book."

Ed stared at her. There had to be some kind of punch line, some trick she was playing on him that he wasn't getting. This would mark the second time in a week that Heather Gannis had invited Ed Fargo over to her apartment. And that hadn't happened in . . . well, in forever.

"Going once," she joked, snatching the movie back. "Going twice . . ."

Hmmm. Ed glanced down at his watch, then over at the exit. Gaia was now officially an hour late. Maybe he should go. She would understand if he decided to bolt. Besides, if she missed him here, she would feel so guilty that she'd have no choice but to go to Victoria's party. He'd call her when he got to Heather's.

When I get to Heather's.

Just saying the words to himself sent a strange sensation through his insides. It was almost like déjà vu. Here he was with Heather in their old video store, laughing and hanging out as if nothing had changed. As if he weren't in a wheelchair. As if she weren't going out with Sam Moon. (And why *wasn't* she with Sam tonight, anyway?) As if she hadn't

37

dumped Ed after his accident because she couldn't deal with the horrible tragedy of it all—

"Going three times . . ."

As if Gaia Moore had never entered their lives.

"Deal," Ed said.

I LOOK LIKE DEATH.

A Figure of Speech

Gaia stared at her horrific reflection in the bathroom mirror. Well, maybe death was a slight exaggeration. She looked like she'd been hit by a car. Funny: That was a figure of speech, wasn't it? *"Jesus—what happened to you? You look like you were hit by a car."* Ha ha ha.

Maybe it wasn't so funny.

Her hair was matted with dried, caked blood. Bloody scratches ran up and down the right side of her body: her palm, elbow, shin, shoulder. . . . There was a cut on her right cheek.

But that wasn't the worst of it. She could deal with her physical injuries. They were relatively minor. Nothing was broken. Her flesh burned; her body ached—but the agony was tolerable. Any amount of physical agony was tolerable. Shutting out pain was a lesson she'd learned from her father long ago. For some perverse reason, the absence of the fear gene seemed to make pain all the more excruciating, but that was the price of being a freak.

No . . . the worst of it was that she'd freaked out and abandoned Sam.

She drew in a deep, quivering breath. Her thoughts swirled like water in a toilet bowl. She'd had a very good reason for abandoning Sam, hadn't she? Yes . . . but it wasn't one that she could share with Sam—or even fully articulate to herself. Because in the brief instant that she'd hurled herself in front of that car to save Sam's life, she'd imagined that she saw somebody familiar behind the wheel.

Very familiar.

A fizz of energy shot through her veins—the energy that came in place of fear. It couldn't be true. She'd dreamed the whole thing up. Obviously the trauma of the accident had triggered some kind of strange psychological reaction. An instantaneous reaction.

I saw my dad.

Of course it wasn't. It could have more easily been her mysterious uncle. But her instincts screamed that it wasn't her uncle; it was her dad.

Her throat clenched. She stared hard at her face in the mirror. Her pupils were two black holes. Empty.

There were no answers there. Either she had seen him or . . . she hadn't. But if—

"Gaia?" Ella's voice shattered her thoughts.

Oh, please. "What?" she yelled.

"Is everything okay?" came the muffled question.

Gaia frowned. As if Ella even cared. What was *with* her today? Why couldn't she just drop the concerned-mom act? It was even more nauseating than the doting wife she played with George.

"Gaia?"

"Everything's *fine,*" she snapped.

There was a pause. "Well, okay . . . I'm just stepping out for a minute to get some wine for dinner. All right?"

"Knock yourself out," Gaia muttered.

She shook her head and turned away from her reflection. This whole day was beginning to freak her out:

She was hallucinating—seeing her father while being mown down by a car.

Ella was pretending to care.

Sam was hanging out by her house.

Gaia swallowed. What was that about, anyway? Maybe Sam had come to tell her that he'd broken up with Heather. Maybe he'd come to explain all the weird stuff that happened between them, to forgive her for acting like such a bitch the last time he'd seen her, and to tell her he wanted to hang out, just go to a movie or something—

"Oh, no!" she cried out loud.

Movie. She thought of Ed, sitting alone in the Blockbuster, fuming as he waited for Gaia to show up. Her bruised shoulders sagged. Well. This was just great. Not only did she look like shit—she felt like it, too.

"SO WHAT DO YOU THINK?" HEATHER

Bitch Supreme

asked. "Should we go with pizza or popcorn?"

Ed shrugged. "Um . . . actually, I'm not really all that hungry," he mumbled.

Heather opened her mouth, then closed it. Maybe inviting Ed over here wasn't the greatest idea. He looked so odd, sitting *next* to the couch in his wheelchair—not *on* it with her. The last time he'd been here, a few days ago, they'd avoided the living room altogether. They'd stuck to the kitchen. In retrospect, Heather realized it was probably because of the memories associated with this particular room. *Especially* this particular couch. They had always used to snuggle into the big, soft brown cushions, arms and legs intertwined . . . as close as they could be. It was kind of ironic, in a way: They used to spend evenings here under the guise of "watching movies." At least that's what they'd told Heather's parents. Needless to say, they rarely took the movies out of their boxes.

But this time they *would* watch the movie.

Heather gulped painfully.

Ed was staring at the blank screen, fidgeting.

"Ed, what's wrong?" Heather murmured. "Is being here bumming you out?"

He shook his head and cast a quick smile at her, then lowered his eyes. "No, no, it's not that at all. I've always loved your mom's tacky neopostmodern artwork."

Heather smirked. Good old Ed. At least he could be counted on to use humor as a defense mechanism. *That* hadn't changed.

"So what is it?" she asked.

He turned to her again, then drew in his breath. His expression was hard to read—tentative, almost. "Well, for one thing, I'm going to have to see my sister on Sunday," he said. "Which I'm definitely *not* psyched about."

Heather's eyes narrowed. "Victoria? Why do you have to see her? What's going on?"

Ed shrugged. "She's getting married."

"*Really?*" Heather exclaimed. "On *Sunday?*"

"No, the engagement party's on Sunday. I don't know when the wedding is." He flashed her a sardonic grin. "Hopefully I'll be out of the country or in jail when it happens."

Heather laughed, but she felt a pang of discomfort. She knew all about the bitterness Ed harbored toward his sister. She didn't blame him, either. After all, Victoria had pretty much abandoned Ed after the accident. She'd stayed away from her own brother because she didn't know how to deal with him.

Just like Heather herself.

The discomfort grew. She and Victoria had a lot in common, now that Heather thought about it. They were both very social. No, that was too kind. They were both *snobs*. And they both had run from Ed Fargo when he was no longer cool to be seen with.

She thrust these thoughts from her mind. There was no point. What was done was done. Besides, Victoria wasn't *really* the issue here. His sister's engagement party might be bumming him out—but something else was bothering him, too. Something more immediate. He couldn't stay still. His fingers drummed on the armrests of his wheelchair.

"So what's the other problem?" she asked.

He looked at her, then looked away. "Promise you won't get mad?"

"Oh, Jesus." Heather groaned, slouching back into the cushions. "We're not in the seventh grade anymore. Of course I won't get mad. You can tell me anything."

She meant it, too. In spite of everything that had

happened between them since the accident, she still felt an ease with Ed that she'd never experienced with anyone before or since. Certainly not with her *current* boyfriend—as painful as that was to admit to herself. With Sam she never felt like she could truly let her guard down, as if she could say or do whatever she pleased. But with Ed, she could. There was nothing forced between them, no pretension.

"I was supposed to meet Gaia," he said.

Heather's face shriveled in disgust. It wasn't even a conscious reaction; it was more of a reflex—like jerking your leg after you got hit on the knee with a mallet. *Gaia Moore.* Of course. The bitch supreme. The one who seemed to dominate everyone's thoughts: Ed's, Sam's . . . What the hell did they *see* in her, anyway? Couldn't they tell she was bad news? Her best friend—that girl, Mary—had just been *murdered*, for God's sake. If there was a clearer sign to stay away from somebody, Heather couldn't think of one. Gaia had almost gotten Heather herself killed by those idiot Nazi skinheads back in September. But Ed had somehow conveniently forgotten about that. It was something he and Sam had in common.

Ed sighed. "I knew you'd get mad."

All at once Heather regretted making such an obvious display of her emotions. She wasn't going to let

Gaia Moore ruin her and Ed's time. No way. That had happened more than enough times already. She shook her head and sat up straight, collecting herself. "I'm not mad," she lied. "It's just . . . I don't know. Do you want to leave? Do you want to go meet her?"

"No," Ed replied. He shook his head adamantly. "She was supposed to meet me at Blockbuster, but she never showed. It's *her* fault." He flashed her a wry grin. "Anyway, I'm having fun here. You know, forcing awkward conversation and everything."

Heather's face softened a little. She peered at him closely, trying to determine whether or not he was telling the whole truth. "So what's the problem?" she asked.

"I was just thinking. . . ." Ed chewed his lip and ran a hand through his dark hair (which was still strangely sexy—in that rebellious, juvenile-delinquent kind of way). "Maybe I should call her. You know, just to see if she's all right." He glanced up at her. "Would that be cool?"

"Sure," Heather answered automatically. She shrugged. But part of her wanted to scream. Another part wanted to slap Ed in the face. If there was one thing Heather was certain of, it was that Gaia Moore was fine. Oh, yes. Gaia Moore was always fine, even though those around her died or wallowed in misery.

Ed's eyes remained fixed on hers. "You know,

Heather, I'm really psyched you invited me over," he said softly. "I mean it."

Heather blinked. She felt a strange heat in her chest. Her eyes began to sting. *Oh, Christ. I better not start crying.* First she was pissed at Ed. Then the very next moment she wanted to burst into tears and hug him. Not even Sam had that effect on her.

But Sam didn't have Ed's vulnerability. Strangely enough, he didn't have Ed's toughness, either. Or the same honesty. It was the combination that made Ed so compelling. So unique. Only Ed would admit to worrying about Gaia in the presence of Heather. It was infuriating and admirable all at once.

"I'm really psyched you came," she finally forced herself to reply. Her voice was strained. "It's been so long—"

The phone rang.

Heather sighed. Her gaze locked with Ed's. The two of them laughed.

"Maybe that's Gaia now," she muttered sarcastically, pushing herself out of the couch.

"If it is, tell her to bring a pizza," Ed called after her as she headed to the kitchen.

Now, that would be funny, Heather thought. She grabbed the phone off the wall.

"Hello?"

"It's Mom."

Heather frowned. Her mother's voice was tight,

breathless. Most times she at least said hi. An anxious little knot gathered at the bottom of Heather's stomach.

"Hey," she said cautiously. "What's up?"

"I'm at the hospital."

"*What?*" Heather hissed.

"It's . . . it's your sister," her mother answered, choking on her words.

The knot exploded into full-fledged panic. Heather tried to swallow, gripping the phone tightly. The kitchen seemed to turn black. "What about her?"

"I . . . I don't want to get into it on the phone. Just come as soon as you can, okay? We're at St. Vincent's. In the emergency room." There was a click, and the line went dead.

The emergency room. The words barely registered. Heather shook her head. This was impossible. This wasn't happening.

Phoebe was in the hospital.

"Heather?" Ed's voice floated from the living room. "Is everything all right?"

Heather slammed down the phone and rushed through the living room to the front hall. "Ed, I'm— uh, I'm really sorry," she stammered, without turning around to look at him. She felt like she was fighting her way through a thick haze, as if she was caught in some hallucinatory nightmare. Everything in the apartment suddenly looked too bright, off-kilter, *wrong.* She snatched her coat from the closet and opened the door. "I've gotta go. But you can watch the movie if you—"

"What is it, Heather?" Ed interrupted. "What's wrong?" His voice rose. "Tell me. *Tell* me, Heather!"

"I can't," she whispered.

She closed the door behind her before he could respond. Then she started running. She ran fast as she could, bolting for the fire stairs so that Ed couldn't follow, fighting back tears the whole way.

ELLA WAS LATE.

This was nothing new, of course. She'd been late for a lot of appointments lately. And if there was one deficiency that Loki couldn't tolerate, it was chronic lateness. He had good reasons.

Excellent Motivators

In his world business transactions depended on precise timing. Even a few seconds' error could spell the difference between life and death, between the gain and loss of millions of dollars . . . between control and chaos.

But more important, chronic lateness was merely a

symptom: the manifestation of deeper problems, ones that were far more insidious. In Ella's case her lateness was a symptom of irresponsibility. Of mood swings. Of increasingly erratic behavior. None of which was tolerable.

Still . . . Ella hadn't outlived her usefulness yet. She was still the one in closest proximity to his precious Gaia. And one day, under Loki's careful tutelage, Gaia would overcome *her* imperfections, *her* mood swings and irresponsible tendencies . . . and stand at his side as the exquisitely trained fighting machine she was always meant to be.

But that would all happen in good time. Patience, as he well knew, was the key to success.

Not coincidentally, patience was another trait that Ella lacked.

He glanced across the sparsely furnished apartment at the door buzzer. As if submitting to his will, it emitted a harsh ring. He strode across the bare wood floor and pressed the talk button.

"Yes?"

"She's here," a gruff voice replied.

"Send her up."

Loki waited by the front door. He didn't want her coming any farther than the foyer. She wouldn't play her foolish games with him tonight. She wouldn't tempt him into bed. She would pay for her lateness.

Seconds later there was a knock on the door. Loki leaned forward and opened it.

"I'm so sorry," Ella began. She looked uncharacteristically sloppy: Her red hair was tousled and damp, and her expensive faux fur coat was rumpled. At the very least, Ella could always be counted on for a pristine appearance. But now it looked like she was failing in *this* department as well. "I couldn't get out of the house any earlier. Gaia would start to wonder if I just took off after she was nearly killed—"

"Gaia has no idea you witnessed the accident," Loki interrupted. "She wouldn't notice anything."

Ella stared back at him, her mouth open, her lips trembling. Loki resisted the urge to slap her hard across the face.

"Did you tell her that you saw what happened?" Loki demanded.

She shook her head.

"And what *did* happen, exactly? Do we know who was driving the car? Do we know why Sam Moon happened to be standing in the middle of the street outside your house? Do we know why Gaia was . . . *nearly . . . killed?*" He brought his face within inches of Ella's own. "Can you answer any of these questions?"

"I—I—," she stuttered.

The terror was there, plain for him to see in her wide eyes. Good. Maybe terror would help get her back on track during the last few weeks of her . . . assignment.

"Well, don't worry," he said, abruptly lightening his tone. He withdrew his head and began pacing around the apartment. "I can answer these questions for myself. But it's a pity you've left me with no choice."

Ella took a step forward. "But I didn't—"

"Silence!" Loki barked. He whirled and thrust an accusing finger at her. "What am I *paying* you for?"

She didn't answer. She simply bowed her head.

"Now go home," Loki commanded. "Don't let Gaia out of your sight."

"I was hoping . . ." She let the sentence hang and lifted her eyes. This time there was fear—but something else as well. The old, familiar spark of seduction. But it was almost *pleading*. And therefore that much more pitiful.

"Go home to your husband," Loki spat.

Ella swallowed. "How can you do this to me?" she murmured.

Loki looked her directly in the eye. "Don't make me repeat myself," he stated, very calmly.

Without another word Ella turned and stormed out of the apartment, slamming the door behind her.

Loki allowed himself a little smile. Maybe he'd get some professionalism now. Yes. Sexual frustration, anger, and fear were all excellent motivators. He'd give Ella one more chance. One last shot at redemption.

Tonight.

From: gaia13@alloymail.com
To: shred@alloymail.com
Time: 6:45 P.M.
Re: Please don't hate me
Hey, Ed—

I've been trying to call your house for the last hour, but nobody's home. I know you're not at the video store, either, because I called there, too . . . anyway, you probably think I'm the biggest loser on the planet, but there's a very good reason I didn't come to meet you. I got hit by a car. Seriously. You'll know I'm telling the truth when you see my face at school on Monday. It kind of put me in a daze for a while. Call or write back as soon as you get this, okay?

—G$

From: gaia13@alloymail.com
To: smoon@alloymail.com
Time: 6:47 P.M.
Re: Sorry for the freak-out

Hi, Sam,

So I just wanted to let you know that I'm really sorry I bolted today on the street. I just didn't want to deal with any ambulances or hospitals or anything like that. Hospitals kind of give me the creeps. I've got a lot of bad memories associated with them. Anyway, I'm okay, in case you were wondering. I just wanted to know if you're okay, too. By the way, what were you doing on Perry Street? I'll understand if you don't want to answer.

                                        —Gaia

From: smoon@alloymail.com
To: gaia13@alloymail.com
Time: 7:05 P.M.
Re: Glad you wrote

Gaia,

Thanks for letting me know you're okay. I'm okay, too. But there's something I want to talk to you about. Can we have dinner tonight? I need to see you. I'll explain everything then. Corner of Waverly and University at nine o'clock.

—Sam

To: smoon@alloymail.com
From: gaia13@alloymail.com
Time: 7:06 P.M.
Re: I'll be there
    See you then.

                      —Gaia

She squeezed
her eyes
tightly shut.
She wouldn't
think about **an**
death. Not **entire**
tonight. **lifetime**

She would
banish death
from existence.

ONE OF THE BENEFITS OF WORKING

with his old friend George was that Tom never had to explain himself if a mission or meeting went awry. George implicitly understood that Tom never had to justify his actions. To *anyone*.

Potential Liability

The agency wasn't as understanding.

It didn't matter, though. Explaining himself was of no concern to Tom now. This wasn't agency business. This was a family matter. The agency couldn't be involved. At this very moment, in fact, his superiors were probably reeling over why he hadn't issued a status report in the last few weeks, why he had simply abandoned his job in Russia and flown to New York. There was a very good chance he would be reprimanded. Or demoted. Or simply neutralized. Three decades of sacrifice and patriotism meant nothing if the agency considered you to be a potential liability. Nothing at all.

I may very well be a marked man.

Then again, he'd been a marked man for as long as he'd been an agent. Every terrorist group from Belfast to Hong Kong had an open contract out on his life. But that came with the territory.

Tom shook thoughts of mortality aside and scanned the deserted alley. The air was bitter cold—

the kind of cold that numbed extremities and bit at exposed flesh. But he was used to it. The weather reminded him of Russia, in fact. Of Moscow.

Of Katia.

Sweet Katia.

Bile rose in his throat. He swallowed the foulness and shook his head. If Katia knew that Loki was hunting their daughter, that Loki wanted to take Gaia away from them, to bring her into his monstrous existence . . . horror wouldn't even begin to describe Katia's emotions. No. Tom had to be strong. He *had* to prevail. For Katia's sake.

Shuffling footsteps tore into Tom's stream of consciousness.

He glanced at his watch, then breathed a sigh of relief. George was right on time. He lifted his eyes to see George's shadowy form in the pale glow of a lone streetlamp, hunched over from the cold. Icy breath drifted from George's mouth in quick puffs.

"How are you, Tom?" he murmured as he approached.

Tom managed a smile for his old friend. "I've had better days. How's Gaia?"

George paused, then took a quick peek around the alleyway. Tom had already combed the area several times, but at their age, security precautions were as instinctive as breathing.

"Pretty banged up, but all right," George finally

answered. "At least from what Ella told me. What happened?"

"I nearly killed my daughter, for starters," Tom mumbled.

George gaped at him. "It was *you?*"

Tom nodded, overcome by a sudden stab of nausea at the memory of Gaia's body flipping over the hood of his car. "Yes," he muttered. "I nearly hit some boy. A boy I recognized . . . I think he's a friend of Gaia's. She saved his life and nearly got herself killed in the process."

"Good God," George hissed. He shook his head, his brow tightly furrowed. "I had no idea. What were you doing on Perry Street?"

"I couldn't find a parking space," Tom replied matter-of-factly.

Their eyes met. A sad smile passed between them.

"I forget that the real world intrudes in our work sometimes," George said wistfully.

Tom shrugged. "So do I."

George's expression grew serious. "So how should we proceed?"

"You tell me. What's the word on Loki?"

"The same," George answered, scanning the alley once more. "Like I told you before, preliminary intelligence indicates that he's got somebody close to Gaia. A plant. That's all we know."

So nothing's changed in two weeks, Tom thought.

Frustration tore at him; he felt like punching the nearby brick wall. But he didn't blame George. The poor man was doing the best he could under the circumstances. Besides, Loki was far too clever to leave himself vulnerable. It was a miracle that George knew as much as he did.

But then a thought occurred to Tom.

"Could the plant be the boy?" he asked.

George shrugged, sighing. "Your guess is as good as mine." He stamped his feet and rubbed his gloved hands together, shivering as a gust of wind swept through the burnt-out tenements.

The streetlamp flickered. Bits of garbage and old newspaper rustled across the old cobblestones. There was nothing more to say. Nothing had changed. Tom could only continue to wait as the situation developed ... and to watch Gaia as closely as possible. It was time to adjourn this meeting. He should let his friend return to the warmth and comfort of his home. Hopefully Gaia would be there, too. Resting. Recuperating. With Ella to help her.

"How's Ella?" Tom asked.

"She's—" George broke off in midsentence. His entire body seemed to sag into his trench coat. "To be honest, I don't know."

Tom shot him a confused stare. "What do you mean?"

"I . . . she—she's been acting odder than usual

recently," he stammered with uncharacteristic clumsiness. He avoided Tom's gaze. "She comes and goes without telling me and keeps hours I don't understand. I . . ." His voice faded, as if he'd suddenly run out of air.

Not good, Tom thought. But he suppressed his alarm. Aside from the fact that George was his most trusted friend, Tom took comfort in the knowledge that George seemed to have such a stable relationship with his beautiful, young photographer wife. Tom had counted on their providing a solid, healthy environment for his daughter, one where she would be nurtured by both a father *and* mother figure.

"It's the stress," Tom stated after a minute—as much for himself as for George. "The stress of trying to get her career off the ground. Photography's a tough business. Especially in this town. Very competitive."

George nodded. "Right," he said, without any conviction.

Tom swallowed, regarding his friend closely. He hadn't noticed before—but George seemed haggard. His skin was very pale. Puffy sacks hung beneath his eyes.

"I'm sorry," Tom murmured.

"It's okay," George answered. He smiled tiredly. "It'll pass. Every relationship suffers ups and downs."

Tom nodded. That statement was truer than

George probably even realized. It certainly applied perfectly to his relationship with Gaia. He extended a hand. "If there's anything I can—"

"Don't worry," George interrupted. His voice caught. "I'll make it work." His jaw twitched, but he looked Tom in the eye. "For Gaia's sake."

WHEN HEATHER FIRST STEPPED INTO

Concentration Camp Victim

the cold and antiseptic-smelling intensive care ward, her first reaction was one of rage. Pure rage. Staring down at Phoebe's skeletal frame—the way she was hooked up to all those IVs, lying under the blankets and sickly green hospital robes as if she were already a corpse—Heather wanted to wring Phoebe's neck. To scream. To tear Phoebe's beautiful brown hair from her scalp.

You idiot! How could you let this happen? How could you do this to yourself?

But she didn't. She kept her mouth shut. Because Heather knew if she tried to speak, she would very likely start bawling like an infant.

"I can't believe we didn't see this coming," her mother whispered at her side.

Heather swallowed and shook her head. *Right,* she thought bitterly. Maybe part of her anger had to do with the guilt that was presently shredding her insides. Heather *had* seen this coming. Only last week she'd found herself gaping in shock at Phoebe's naked body, fresh from the shower—at those protruding eye sockets, at all the bones that jutted sharply from beneath her pallid and anemic flesh. Heather had even gone so far as to comment on how thin her sister looked. *Too* thin. Heather had seen something like this coming and done nothing to stop it.

Now Phoebe's body was so starved, so deprived of nutrients that it simply wouldn't function. It had shut down, like a toy that had run out of batteries.

Of course, toys didn't have souls. They didn't look like concentration camp victims, either. They didn't need life-support systems just to keep their frail hearts beating—

"Maybe you should go home, Heather," her mother whispered.

"No," Heather croaked. She shook her head again, violently. She'd only been here twenty minutes. She had no intention of leaving. Not until Phoebe gave her some kind of sign—*anything*—to prove that she was still with them. And a pulsating beep or a blip on a screen didn't count. No way. Phoebe had to say something.

To open her eyes, if only for a second. Even the mere lifting of a finger would be enough.

The door opened behind them.

Heather glanced over her shoulder. A short, balding doctor in a white lab coat stood there, holding a clipboard.

"I'm very sorry," he murmured with a sympathetic smile. "You're going to have to wait outside now. We need to run a few more tests." He gestured down the hall

Heather exchanged a quick glance with her mother. Her throat caught. In the sickly blue glow of the fluorescent lights, she couldn't help but be struck by the resemblance between Phoebe and Mom. Both had those same deep-set eyes, the same mouth . . . only Mom's lips were full and red, whereas Phoebe's were cracked and nearly white. Mom's arms didn't look like you could snap them with two fingers. A network of purplish veins weren't bulging beneath translucent skin. Heather shot a quick glance back toward her sister.

"Of course," Mom said.

She took Heather gently by the arm, steering her toward an orange vinyl couch out in the long hallway. Heather nearly collapsed into the cushions. She hadn't realized how exhausted she was. The simple act of sitting was like settling into a warm tub. She stretched her legs and yawned. She'd been on her feet ever since she'd gotten the phone call. Of course, maybe only an hour had passed, but it already seemed like an entire lifetime.

It might just well be an entire lifetime.

She squeezed her eyes tightly shut. She wouldn't think about death. Not tonight. She would banish death from existence.

After a minute or so, when she was certain her mind was clear, she allowed her eyelids to flutter open.

Her mom sat beside her, rigid—her bleary eyes pinned on the door that was now closed.

Intensive Care Unit:
Authorized Personnel Only Beyond This Point

"Are you sure you don't want to go—"

"I'm *sure*, Mom," Heather interrupted, sounding harsher than she intended. "I want to stay here. I'll be fine."

Fortunately her mother just nodded, too tired to argue.

Heather glanced at a snack machine down the hall. Nah. She was in no mood for a sticky candy bar. She didn't have an appetite. The thought of food was . . . well, she didn't know *what* it was.

Her mother started rummaging through her purse. "The doctor gave me something," she said absently. "I thought you might want to take a look at it. . . ." She pulled out a crumpled pamphlet and handed it to Heather.

A Parents' Guide to Anorexia Nervosa

Perfect, Heather thought dismally. Just the thing to

take her mind off Phoebe. A little light reading before bed. She scowled at her mother—but her mom had already curled up into a fetal position at the edge of the couch and closed her eyes.

So. This was great. Here she was in a hospital, with her mom passed out and her sister near death. A hell of a Friday night, wasn't it? Maybe she *should* take a look at this thing. It was just too bad it wasn't called *A Sister's Guide*. But the advice could probably extend to all family members. She opened to the front page and began to read.

Anorexia is characterized by a significant weight loss resulting from excessive dieting.

Duh . . . news flash. Heather rolled her eyes.

Women are often motivated by both an intense desire to be thin and an intense fear of becoming obese. If they are successful at losing weight, people take note, complimenting them on their appearance and reinforcing the weight loss pattern.

Another statement of the obvious. Everyone: Mom, Dad, Heather herself, even Ed . . . all of them wouldn't shut up about how great Phoebe looked when she came home from college. But in a matter of a month Phoebe had gone from diminutive to diminished to destroyed. The most amazing part of it was how clueless they all were. Then again, who would *want* to believe that Phoebe was committing slow suicide before their very eyes?

The denial made sense, though, in a way. Phoebe

had looked great . . . up to a point. And in the Gannis household appearance was everything. It was the highest priority, in fact: whether it was the appearance of a perfect family or the appearance of living the way they lived before the money was gone—

Heather winced. This pamphlet was leading to places she didn't really want to go. She flipped ahead a few pages.

Anorexics are usually dutiful daughters who set very high standards for themselves, striving for perfection.

Jesus. The more she read, the more it seemed Phoebe was a poster girl for anorexia. She was a good student. She was organized. She went to a fine college. And compared to Heather, she hardly ever talked back to their mother. In fact, their mom had told Heather more than once to look to Phoebe as an example.

Right.

So with all that going for her, why the hell was Phoebe starving herself?

Heather's jaw tightened. She could feel the rage returning. Phoebe had brought this on *herself.* Her eyes flashed back down to the page.

Eating disorders are diseases that provide the illusion of control. Anorexics believe that while they can't control life, they can control their weight.

But as quickly as the rage swelled, it subsided. The need to feel in control, to *be* in control, was something Heather could definitely relate to. She certainly had her own control issues. With Sam, for example.

Specifically, with sleeping with him. Looking back on it now, she realized sex had been a ploy on her part—an empty, manipulative act to gain the upper hand in their relationship. The thought of it made her sick. God, she had even lied, telling him that her first time with him was her first time *ever*. Her stomach turned. She'd been dishonest with him, with herself, with the world. She'd been playing a role, trying to figure out what Sam was looking for, who he wanted her to be—or who she *thought* he wanted her to be—and she did everything she could to become that girl. . . .

And what had it accomplished? Did Sam love her any better for all her lies? No, of course not. Their relationship had deteriorated to the point of being hard to recognize as a relationship at all. On some level, Sam probably sensed her dishonesty and hated her for it. Almost as much as she hated herself.

A tear fell from her cheek, splattering on the wrinkled page.

The only possible comfort in Sam's rejection was the fact that he wasn't rejecting her raw, true self. Sam had never even met that girl.

Ed Fargo was the only guy who'd had that pleasure.

It was a strange, strange thing about life. She worked so hard trying to keep it in control, and yet her few genuinely happy times came when she let go of it completely.

Sam Moon.

It's a name I say to myself
almost every hour of every day.
Sam Moon. I can see his face
before me: that chiseled jaw, that
smooth skin, those pensive eyes.
Sam Moon. Even the sound of it is
magical. The delicate slither of
the *S*, flowing over the *a* and *m*
into the smooth *oo*. . . . It's
like an incantation. A spell. The
two words that keep me sane.

If Loki only knew how I har-
nessed Sam Moon's passions, how I
controlled him on that night,
then Loki would treat me with the
respect I deserve. But he will
someday. I'm sure of it. Sam Moon
is my greatest triumph. A verita-
ble work of art. Compared to
those teenage sleazebags in the
park . . . but there isn't really
a comparison, is there?

And at some point in the not-
so-distant future, Loki will
find out what I accomplished.
He'll tremble at my power to
manipulate. Until he does, I'll

keep Sam Moon under my thumb.

But I'll never truly let him go, either. Loki may have most of my heart, but not all of it. Sam Moon owns a little piece of it now, too. Forever. I'll always keep him close to me—and not only for the unspoken bond between us.

No. I'll keep him close to me because he'll always remind me how I defeated Gaia Moore.

The *Raging Predinner Internal Debate:*

It's a Date

1. He asked me out.
2. I took a shower.
3. I tried on three outfits.
4. It's just the two of us.
5. It's dinner.
6. He wants to talk about something really important.

No, It Isn't

1. It was an e-mail.
2. I took the shower before I got the e-mail.
3. They were all the same. All I own are T-shirts and cargo pants.
4. He isn't picking me up.
5. He has a girlfriend (who I hate).
6. Maybe he's going to propose to Heather and needs advice about what kind of ring to buy, which I—as a girl—can provide.

Even now her body ached to be next to his. To feel his **something** breath on her neck. To **inane** lose herself in that powerful embrace.

THE WHOLE SCENARIO WAS SHAMEFUL.

Completely and utterly shameful. But Sam was beyond caring. All that mattered now was that Gaia heard the truth. Besides, Sam had learned to live with self-loathing.

Despicable, Cowardly Rat

He'd learned to live with an indescribable emptiness because he knew that he had nobody to blame but himself.

The real kicker was that this meeting should have been perfect. He shook his head, sniffing the frigid night air, and glanced into the abyss of Washington Square Park. It was nearly deserted. The paths were shadowed by leafless trees. But the miniature Arc de Triomphe down the block was all lit up, jutting from the wintry landscape like a giant, glowing tombstone. Soon Gaia would be appearing out from under it.

Yup. This should have been perfect.

Everything was in place. He'd invited Gaia out to a late dinner on a Friday night, and she'd accepted. So if he'd done what he'd been supposed to do—meaning if he'd behaved like a decent, moral human being instead of a despicable, cowardly rat—then this could have been the beginning of a new chapter in his life. He could have taken Gaia out for a romantic dinner, then invited her back to his dorm room. . . .

But no.

That wouldn't happen. Instead of dumping Heather, he'd avoided her. Instead of running away from Ella, he'd slept with her—simultaneously cheating on his *real* girlfriend and having sex with the foster mother of his *real* love. Sam wasn't a religious guy by any means, but still, he couldn't help wonder: Exactly how many sins had he committed in that one heinous act? Enough to land him front row seats in the fiery pit of hell for all eternity—that was for damn sure. Then again, maybe he was in hell already.

Strange. For somebody who was so good at chess, at *decisive* maneuvering, he'd made a mess of his life. On the other hand, it was unfair to compare a chessboard to the streets of New York City. You knew where you stood on a chessboard. You knew what the rules were. Here, out in the coldness and darkness and confusion, you pretty much had to make up the rules as you went along. Too bad Sam was no good at improvising.

"Sam?"

He jumped at the sound of Gaia's voice. She'd come from behind him—from the direction of Broadway, catching him totally off guard.

"Uh, hey," he mumbled, struggling to collect himself. Even in the freezing cold, with her nose red and her cheek freshly scarred from today's car accident, Gaia was still beautiful. The bruises and scratches on her face only added to her mystique . . . her paradoxical aura of both strength and vulnerability. She stood before him, shivering in her ratty overcoat, her blond hair flapping in the wind from under her wool cap.

Staring at her made him feel sick.

How could I have betrayed you like that? he wondered for the hundredth time. Of course, he'd justified the betrayal to himself by rationalizing: It *wasn't* a real betrayal. Technically he didn't have a relationship with Gaia—except for a few moments here and there, a fleeting kiss at a time when she was basically concussive, and a lot of other strange encounters. . . .

"Are you okay?" Gaia asked in the silence.

"Huh?" He shook his head, then forced an awkward smile. "Uh, yeah."

Gaia gazed into his eyes. "Did the accident shake you up?"

He shrugged. "A little," he said. Actually, the truth was that he was a lot more shaken up just standing right here, talking to her. "So . . . uh, where do you feel like eating?" he asked lamely.

"Anywhere," she mumbled. She glanced over her shoulder. "So long as it's not on Broadway."

Sam frowned. "Why's that?"

Gaia turned back toward him, then laughed grimly. "I just don't want to run into my foster mother. I caught a glimpse of her on West Fourth Street." She shook her head, wrinkling her nose as if she'd smelled something foul. "It was weird. It was almost like she was following me or something."

"Are you serious?" Sam cried. *Shit.* His pulse picked up a notch. He stood on his tiptoes, peering over Gaia's shoulders toward the lights of Broadway. But the street was nearly deserted—except for a few heavily bundled up college kids.

"Yeah." Gaia's face was twisted in confusion. "What's the matter?"

"Nothing," Sam lied. He took her arm and started hustling her across the street toward the park. No way could he let Ella interfere in this . . . confession. There was no telling what she'd say or do. Sam had to tell Gaia the truth *his* way so that at least he'd have a chance of making her understand the situation from his point of view. "So, um . . . uh, I was thinking—I was thinking about going to the . . . the Olive Tree Café," he sputtered. "Have you ever been there?"

Gaia gently extricated herself from his grip. For the briefest instant he felt an electric tingle as her flesh touched his. But it faded the instant their gazes locked.

"Are you sure you're okay?" she demanded.

The two of them paused on the opposite corner. Sam couldn't keep his eyes from flitting back toward Broadway. He had a clean view of all of Waverly Place, and it was now completely empty. He breathed a secret sigh of relief. Maybe she'd given up and gone on to stalk some *other* college-age chump.

"There's something you aren't telling me," Gaia stated.

Sam's gaze flashed back to her. Now his pulse was in overdrive. He took a deep breath, suddenly acutely aware of the ticking seconds, of the freezing cold, of every sensation . . . then he realized something. Something inane, actually. The right-front pocket of his jeans was empty. He slapped at it—but there was nothing there. His wallet. *Jesus*. In all his freaking out about Gaia, he'd left his wallet back in his dorm room.

"Actually, there is," he blurted out. "I just realized I don't have my wallet. Wait here, okay? I'll be right back."

Gaia's jaw dropped. She looked pissed. "Wait here? But . . ."

Before she could finish, he whirled and dashed up University Place toward Eleventh Street. The rat was on the run again. Procrastination, memory loss, and chickening out came in pretty handy sometimes.

A Monument to Human Filth

doubt at all in Gaia's mind. This was definitely *not* a date. A guy just didn't bolt from a girl and leave her standing in the freezing cold if he was taking her out. She scowled and bounced up and down on the balls of her feet, trying to keep warm. Why didn't he just ask her to come with him? What was he so *scared* of, anyway? Gaia used to think that she'd never wish the fearlessness gene on anyone—even her worst enemy—but now she took it back. She would have happily loaned it to Sam for a few seconds at least, so he'd just spit out whatever he had to say and be done with it.

She wrapped her arms around herself and glanced into the park. A peculiar numbness tugged at her stomach. Asking her to meet him *here* was a pretty thoughtless decision, too. The memories associated with Washington Square Park didn't exactly fill Gaia with the warm fuzzies. Mary had been shot here less than two weeks ago. People got killed here all the time, in fact. Or so it seemed.

The danger was what she used to love about this place . . . the feeling that anything could happen at any time. Now the uncertainty just made her depressed.

The park was a monument to human filth, to people's worst impulses: to the desire to kill, to rape, to hustle, to poison one another's bodies with drugs.

Her gaze roved over the barren tree limbs, over the rusted iron fences and frozen lawns. What *was* it about this place that drew people here, anyway? It was a dump. But even now—even at night in the freezing cold—people were hanging out. Three burly guys in leather jackets were walking out of the shadows right now, in fact. Gaia sneered. Maybe they were some of Skizz's old clients, looking to score some coke. Maybe they hadn't heard the news yet. Well. Gaia could perform a public service and tell them that Skizz was out of commission. Permanently.

Wait a second.

The three guys were walking right toward her. They slowed as they drew closer.

Gaia's eyes narrowed.

They were staring at her.

No doubt about it. Three pairs of hard eyes were fixed on her own. A burst of warmth suddenly shot through her limbs, as if an electric light had been turned on inside her. She felt no fear, of course—but she did feel curiosity. And readiness. Who were these guys? They didn't look like druggies. No . . . their bodies were too thick, too healthy. They looked more like cops. Or security guards. And their faces were oddly unremarkable. None of them had any striking or distinguishing features. They could have been brothers, triplets—born to an utterly nondescript family. . . .

She drew in her breath.

They stopped right in front of her.

Now, *this* was strange.

None of them moved. Okay. It was more than strange—it was highly surreal. What the hell did they want? They didn't look menacing, or threatening . . . or anything. Their expressions were utterly dead. She felt like she was standing in front of a semicircle of three statues.

"Uh . . . can I help you with something?" she asked, very calmly.

The one in the middle nodded. "Yes," he said in a toneless voice. "As a matter of fact, you can."

IT'S A GODDAMNED FRIDAY NIGHT,

Bored Beyond Belief

Ella thought, furiously slurping a double latte. She shifted on the hard Starbucks stool and glared through the huge window at the

Broadway street scene. So many hip young passersby. So many couples. All looking so smug and content. And why not? They were all on their way to someplace exciting, someplace to let loose. Yet here *she* was—bored beyond belief.

It's a goddamned Friday night, and I'm wasting it by following some psycho teenage girl around.

It had to be freezing cold, too. Her fingers felt like they were about to fall off. Even the warmth of the coffee cup did little to soothe them. Her hands were red and chapped and . . . ugly. *Her* hands. She'd probably catch hypothermia. Her winter wear wasn't designed for long-term exposure to the elements. No, it was designed for style, to make her look good during those brief moments when she was caught outside. When she was hailing a cab, for instance. Or when she stepped from a cab into a party or club.

But then, when was the last time she had *been* to a party or club?

Not in years. *Years!* She took another sip of the coffee, burning her tongue. Her eyes smoldered. She was young; she was beautiful—and time was slipping away. She wouldn't be young and beautiful forever. Why couldn't Loki make whatever move he was planning to make and put an end to all this nonsense?

She deserved a *medal* for her patience. For putting

up with George . . . that sniveling, pathetic wimp. For following Loki's every command. Most of all, for living with Gaia Moore. For not *killing* Gaia Moore.

Her fingers tightened around the paper cup. As much as Loki enraged her, she couldn't control her feelings. Even now her body ached to be next to his. To feel his breath on her neck. To lose herself in that powerful embrace. To be . . . complete. But if Loki wouldn't accommodate her, then she'd just have to find somebody else to satisfy those needs. Just in the interim.

A secret smile crossed her lips.

You don't exactly hate it, do you, Ella?

No. She didn't. She loved it. And a woman needed her diversions. Abruptly she tossed the half-finished latte into the garbage and stood. She'd had just about enough of following Gaia around for the night. Besides, the freak was headed for the park—to play chess with those ridiculous characters, or to vandalize the place, or to do whatever the hell it was she did there. Frankly, Ella didn't care. Loki was wasting both her time *and* his by forcing her to keep an eye on Gaia.

But what he didn't know wouldn't hurt him. Because now Ella was going to have a little fun. Oh, yes. She smiled again as she fished her cell phone out of her pocket and left the coffee shop.

GAIA BURST OUT LAUGHING AS THE

Seven Zillion to One

middle guy stepped forward and threw a punch straight at her face. She couldn't help it. It was just so *absurd.* Every single time she walked into this park, somebody tried to pick a fight with her. Every single time. What were the odds of that? Seven zillion to one? True, she sometimes went *looking* for fights. But why did fights naturally look for her?

The fist whizzed with an inch of Gaia's face as she stepped back.

Too slow, asshole.

She spun and crouched into a kung fu stance, sizing up each of them. If they wanted to get their asses kicked, fine. It would be her pleasure. A strange combination of weariness and adrenaline coursed through her veins. What a drag. She really didn't want to have to go through this tonight. *Really.*

Luckily, the laughter seemed to catch the three morons off guard. That gave her an immediate advantage. No time to waste. Middle Guy was still leaning off balance from the missed connection. She lashed out and kicked him in the kneecap.

"Ahh!" he screamed. He dropped from her field of vision.

Her gaze immediately shifted to Left Guy. He was crouched in a kung fu stance, just like hers. He might be a more capable opponent. Better save him for last. Middle Guy writhed on the pavement. Gaia's eyes flashed to Right Guy. He was coming straight at her, throwing a punch with his left arm. *Can't you do better than that?* she wondered, laughing again. It was another telegraphed strike, easy to deflect. She shifted to the right and grabbed the guy's arm, simultaneously kicking his shin with a swift toe strike. The force of his own momentum instantly flipped him in midair.

"No—"

His skull struck the pavement first—hitting with a sickening *thwok*—and he rolled over with a groan.

Two down.

All of Gaia's nerves were tingling as she turned her attention to Left Guy. Her entire body was burning, pulsing, on fire with the heat of combat. She forced herself to laugh once more, just to instill fear in him. Fear was the greatest weapon. But his face was a blank mask. Oh, well. He'd be scared of her soon enough.

And hopefully by the time she'd finished him off, Sam would have found his freaking wallet.

"COME ON, COME ON," SAM GRUNTED under his breath.

He whirled around his closet-size dorm room, flinging papers and books and clothing everywhere—but he still couldn't find it. He

Whiny, Little-Girl Voice

paused for a moment, breathing heavily. This method of searching was no good. He was just making it harder on himself. His room looked like a blast zone. But he had left it here, hadn't he? He had been positive it would be sitting right on top of his desk. . . .

Pockets. Right. He had to check all of his pockets.

With one eye still scanning the mess, he snatched a pair of jeans from the floor and tore through them. Nope. His breathing quickened. He tossed the pair aside. *This is bad; this is bad. . . .* Gaia was probably getting more pissed by the second. He tossed the jeans aside and grabbed another pair. Not in there, either. Well, at the very least he could console himself with knowing that no matter how pissed she got now, it would be nothing compared to how pissed she'd be later—

The phone rang.

He swallowed. That was probably her, calling to tell him to forget about dinner and to go screw himself.

He dropped the second pair of jeans and lunged for the phone, nearly tripping over a mountain of laundry.

"Hello?" he gasped.

"Hey, there," a sultry voice whispered.

Ella. The blood drained from his face. His hands went clammy. "What the hell do you want?" he hissed.

"What's wrong, baby?" she murmured in a whiny, little-girl voice. It filled him with revulsion. "I was hoping I could drop by to talk to you—"

"Don't call me '*baby*,'" he snapped. "I'm not your baby."

There was a pause. "What's wrong?" she asked.

"You are!" he shouted. His face reddened. "Can't you just *leave me alone!*"

She giggled. "I love it when young men get angry. It's such a turn-on."

Sam blinked. He couldn't believe this. Talking to her was like talking to an alien. "What do you *want*, Ella?"

"I want *you*," she whispered.

"Well, that's not going to happen." He forced himself to take a deep breath to try to maintain some semblance of control. "But you know . . . actually, it's a good thing you called. Because now I can tell you what I came by to tell you today. I never, ever want to see you again."

Ella clucked her tongue. "I don't believe you," she stated.

His eyes widened. Incredible. Maybe she *was* an alien. "Well, *start* believing," he growled. "Because I'm sick of this. I don't want your calls. I don't want your e-mail. I don't want to hear your name or even *think* about you—"

"Why?" she interrupted. "Because of Gaia?"

Hot pain stabbed into his chest. "Leave her out of this," he warned.

Ella chuckled. "You know, I don't think that's such a good idea anymore. I think she should be in on everything. It's only fair—"

"If you tell her anything, I'll kill you," he whispered between tightly clenched teeth. A red haze filled his brain. His voice quavered. He gripped the phone so tightly that his knuckles turned bone white. "I mean it."

"No, you—"

He slammed the phone down on the hook. All at once he felt psychotic, out of control. His breath came fast. He was practically hyperventilating. Maybe he should just go find her. Maybe he should just get a knife, or a gun, or *something*—and shut her up for good. But even as these twisted thoughts swirled through his brain, he knew what he had to do. He had to get back to Gaia. Wallet or no wallet, he had to talk to her.

Before Ella did.

PUNCH. BLOCK. KICK.

The Strangest Fight

"Hai!"

Gaia withdrew again. Puffs of frozen breath filled the air around her, but she was no longer cold. Her b r a i n hummed, but her body was a cool stone. Once more she and the guy circled each other—hands up, eyes locked, legs bent. This was by far the strangest fight she'd ever been in. It should have been over by now. The other two guys had already dragged themselves away and disappeared into the night. And it wasn't even really like *fighting*. It was more like . . . well, like sparring. Like a practice duel. Like what she and her father used to do for hours on end in her old backyard . . .

Without warning the guy suddenly jumped up and spun at the same time, whipping his right leg around in a roundhouse kick—straight for Gaia's head.

But Gaia ducked it easily. She frowned. She couldn't help but feel that even if she *hadn't* ducked, the kick probably wouldn't have connected, anyway. The guy seemed to slow in midair—just barely—and raise his foot a little.

What the hell is going on? Who are you?

Maybe she should ask him. But she doubted he would answer. His face had remained perfectly inscrutable since he'd first appeared, despite his exertion.

They circled each other again.

Gaia's thoughts raced. Obviously whoever he was, he was highly trained. In fact, his fighting style reminded her of the guy who had killed Mary: controlled, disciplined, but vicious. Maybe *he* was one of Skizz's henchmen, too. It was weird, though. Where did Skizz find these guys? For somebody who had seemingly been such a *loser*—fat and strung out and pathetic—Skizz had sure as hell known some dangerous and powerful people.

And why wasn't this guy trying to finish her off? Why was he prolonging the combat?

Maybe he's toying with me.

If Gaia were able to feel fear, this would certainly be an opportune time for it to kick in. But instead she just felt the usual: a void, partially filled with an intoxicating excitement. This guy *had* to have been hired by Skizz. Retribution from beyond the grave. There was no other possible explanation. Which meant that Skizz had been much smarter and more powerful than she'd suspected. Even though he was dead, people were still coming after her. But they could have just *shot* her. She couldn't begin to guess what this guy's motives were—this guy who kept circling her endlessly, blocking every punch and kick but not really making an effort to fight back. Maybe he wanted to torture her. Maybe he wanted to make her suffer instead of killing her.

"Gaia!"

Sam's voice tore through the night.

Christ. It was about time. Only years of rigorous training prevented her from turning in the direction of Sam's approaching footsteps. Her eyes remained fixed on her opponent. If her focus wavered even for an instant, this guy might just decide to end this little game—and her life in the process. Anything was possible. She couldn't be too careful with him.

But instead the guy just smiled.

She froze in midstep, struck by the sinister contrast between his lips and his eyes. His lips were curved upward, but his eyes remained lifeless. In a way, his expression hadn't changed at all.

"Gaia!" Sam shouted again.

The guy whirled and sprinted away from her, disappearing into the shadows of the park. Within seconds he'd vanished. Silently. Another sure sign of excellent training.

"Hey!" she called. But he was gone. She stood on her tiptoes, straining to see him—but before she knew it, Sam had thrown his arms around her. He squeezed her tightly, choking for breath.

"I ran as fast as I could," he gasped. "I saw that you were in a fight. . . ."

Gaia wanted to answer him, to tell him that she was all right. But she couldn't. Every ounce of energy drained from her body. It seemed to pool on the frozen pavement at her feet. She started to open her mouth . . . only her legs gave out from under her. She pitched forward against Sam's body, thankfully blacking out before she even had a chance to be embarrassed.

IT HAD TAKEN EVERY OUNCE OF TOM'S

self-control not to leap from his new rental car and intervene on his daughter's behalf. But somehow—even from the very moment Gaia had been attacked—he'd known that intervention wouldn't be necessary. She could hold her own, obviously; he'd trained her very well . . . but that wasn't the reason.

Proof Versus Instinct

The reason was because she wasn't in jeopardy. Not seriously, anyway. Her attackers didn't intend to kill her.

The signs were subtle, but it was still clear (from the point of view of a skilled martial artist, anyway) that those men had been *testing* his daughter. Sizing her up. Examining her range, her limits. Her stamina. Tom himself had been subjected to many similar tests when he'd first joined the agency: seemingly random fights that sprang from nowhere, pushing him but never placing him in mortal danger.

Loki.

The name reverberated through Tom's brain like a funeral knell. He swallowed, half expecting his twin brother to leap out from behind the car right now and pump a bullet into his head. There was no doubt in Tom's mind that Loki had been behind Gaia's bizarre little . . . encounter. None at all. In fact, it was confirmation of George's suspicions: that Loki wanted Gaia for himself. This fake fight was Loki's way of making sure that Gaia was everything she'd been brought up to be. Oh, yes. It had his foul name written all over it.

Tom couldn't prove this, of course. But in his profession, proof was almost always impossible to find. He'd always relied on instinct. And instinct had never let him down. Not once. Now Gaia was slumped in the arms of that boy, the one he'd almost killed earlier today. . . .

Sam Moon.

Right. *That* was his name. Of course. God, it *frightened* him the degree to which his emotions shredded his mental capabilities whenever his daughter was involved. He certainly should have made the connection earlier. It was the boy who'd been slashed trying to help Gaia once in the park. The boy who had been kidnapped in order to teach Gaia a lesson. Tom had always assumed he could be trusted. Yes, in fact, Tom had left a package for Sam Moon a couple of months ago—and it had ultimately saved his daughter's life.

Or so Tom had believed.

But maybe Gaia's life had never been in danger at all. And maybe the whole kidnapping act had been a clever ruse. Wouldn't that be just like Loki? To arrange a sequence of events over a long period that would virtually *prove* Sam's loyalty to Gaia? To plant someone so convincing that even *Tom* would believe his innocence? Yes. Loki was ingeniously deceptive. Besides, all Tom needed to do was look at this fight. Sam Moon conveniently disappeared just before the fight started, then reappeared at its conclusion.

Nice coincidence, wasn't it?

Tom slumped back in the driver's seat. Okay. Maybe he was jumping to conclusions. But he reviewed what he knew for certain. He *knew* that Loki had planted somebody near Gaia—somebody with easy access to her. Somebody whom Gaia trusted. Possibly somebody her age, even. A close friend. A boyfriend. *This* boy.

Tom couldn't prove his theory, of course. But then, he seldom could.

To: L
From: BFF
Date: January 12
File: 780808
Subject: ELJ
Location: WHEREABOUTS UNKNOWN

Update: Gaia Moore approached and engaged, per instruction. Performed within acceptable parameters. ELJ did not interfere. Nor was ELJ in vicinity. Subsequent surveillance failed to pinpoint subject's location. Cell phone trace indicates one outgoing phone call to NYU dorm. Advise.

To: BFF
From: L
Date: January 12
File: 780808
Subject: ELJ

Directives: Continue to monitor cell phone use.
Await further instruction.

Well, I finally got my answer. Dinner with Sam definitely wasn't a date. If it was, I probably would have *had* dinner. I wouldn't have regained consciousness on the stoop of the Nivens' house, cold and alone, after some crazy fight that didn't make sense.

But that's my life. One senseless event after another.

For all I know, Sam wasn't even the one that carried me home. For all I know, it could have been one of the guys who attacked me in the first place. Or maybe Ella. Yeah, right. Now *that's* funny. Ella comes strolling down Waverly Place, adjusting her hair and smoothing her pleats—and then, oh, no! Horror of horrors! She sees me in a heap on the ground.

If Ella saw that, she'd probably crack open a bottle of champagne.

Whatever.

I just wish Sam would call.

I've tried calling him, but there's no answer. He should have at least pinned a note to my jacket. *Dear Gaia. Sorry to bolt.*

Tonight is one of those nights when I really hate being such a freak. My lame-ass condition (or whatever you want to call it) knocked me out for ten minutes after that fight. I should have known it was going to happen, too. The harder I fight, the more energy gets sapped. It's like the act of fighting is a giant leech that sucks away at my body and leaves me empty. I should have just run. No . . . I should have just followed Sam back to his dorm when he split to find his wallet.

But that's my life, too. A bunch of should-haves that add up to nothing.

Again he heard
nothing. Not
even a breath.
But that
sleepless
silence
night
betrayed
a terror far
greater than
any words could
express.

HEATHER JERKED AWAKE AT THE

sound of snoring. *Loud* snoring. Like an old man's. She sat up straight and rubbed her bleary eyes, struggling to orient herself. For a moment she had no idea where she was. On a vinyl couch, in a brightly lit

Beautiful Bum

hall . . . *hospital.* Right. Her stomach twisted. She blinked a few times. The glare of the linoleum was way too intense. She glanced at her mother, still curled in the same fetal position beside her, sleeping soundly.

What time is it, anyway? she wondered.

Yawning, she peered at her watch.

Jesus. It was almost four in the morning. She tried to stretch, but her back was stiff and achy.

Another gurgling snore echoed off the cold walls.

Heather's face soured. *Gross.* Why was it that hospital waiting rooms were always filled with the dregs of humanity? She turned toward the sound—

Her eyes bulged. Wait a minute.

Ed was here.

At first she thought her exhausted mind was playing tricks on her. But no, he was there, all right—parked right by the door to the intensive care ward, his body sprawled in his wheelchair, his head thrown back in deep sleep. He must have followed her, snuck in here without her knowing. His face was tilted toward the ceiling. His mouth hung wide open. She could see his teeth. Stringy hair hung in front of his closed eyes. A dried stream of drool stained his chin. She froze in her seat, staring at him. His chest rose slowly from under his sweatshirt, and once again a loud snore erupted from his lips. It sounded like a car engine. Heather couldn't help but giggle. He looked *disgusting*. Like he'd just slept on the street for a week. Like a bum.

He squirmed a little, but he didn't wake up.

Heather's eyes moistened. *A bum. A beautiful bum.* A dozen emotions swirled inside her, but she couldn't sort any of them out. She only knew she couldn't stop smiling. Ed was like some kind of magical appari- tion, here to reassure her and her mother that every- thing was going to be okay. How long had he even been sitting in this miserable hall? Long enough to pass out, obviously.

She giggled again and wiped her eyes.

Ed twitched at the sound of her laughter. He lifted his head and stared directly at her, but she couldn't even tell if he was awake. His eyes were red slits, ringed by dark circles. His pale face was utterly blank.

"Hey," Heather murmured.

The faint beginnings of a crooked smile appeared on his lips. His eyelids fluttered, then closed again. "Hey," he croaked.

"Shhh," Heather whispered. "Go back to sleep."

He mumbled something she couldn't understand. It sounded like: "*Ar-oo-ma.*"

She laughed. She almost wished she had a video camera. People were so funny when they were half asleep. "Shhh, Ed," she whispered gently. "We'll talk later."

"Are you mad?"

That's what he was asking. *My God.* He'd come all the way down to the hospital in the middle of the night—interrupting his life for the sake of the Gannis family, without even disturbing them to let them know that he was *here* . . . and he wanted to know if she was mad. Heather's throat caught.

"Why would I be mad?" she choked out. Her voice was so clogged with emotion that it was unrecognizable to herself.

" 'Cause I wasn't supposed to . . ." His voice trailed off. His head slumped to one side. He was out again.

Because you weren't supposed to what? Heather asked herself. *Care? You're not like that, Ed. You can't help but care. And you're too honest to pretend that you don't. That's what makes you so different from everyone else.*

She shook her head and turned away from him. Yet in spite of the fresh batch of tears that were welling in her eyes, she couldn't help but feel a sense of peace. With Ed here, she knew she'd have the strength to face whatever happened to Phoebe. She wouldn't have to hide anymore.

Off the Hook

"YO, MOON! TURN OFF YOUR GODDAMN ringer!"

Sam sat perfectly still in the middle of his laundry-strewn floor, staring at the phone on his desk. Another shrill ring split the silence.

"Moon!" Fists pounded on the door. "At least take the freaking thing off the hook, won't you?"

Sam winced. Mike Suarez had never sounded so angry before. But then, Sam had never kept him up past four in the morning before, either. This was the seventh time the phone had rung since midnight . . . and he doubted it would be the last. He hadn't answered any of the calls. He couldn't even bring himself to *move*. Thank God the door was closed. He could only guess what he looked like: wearing a pair of flimsy boxer shorts, hair in disarray, shivering but bathed in sweat. Like a lunatic. Somebody who should be removed from society and tossed in a padded room.

Actually, that didn't sound so bad. If he were institutionalized, then he'd never have to face Ella again—

"Unplug that phone or I'm gonna break down this door and unplug it for you!" Mike shouted.

Of course. Sam shook his head. He didn't have to torture himself or his suite mates. He could just unplug the phone. Why hadn't *he* thought of that? *Maybe because I'm losing my mind.* With a grunt he forced himself up and ripped the cord out of the wall in midring.

"Sorry," he called.

Mike didn't answer. He simply stomped away.

Add one more person to the list of people who hate Sam Moon. A bitter smile crossed his face as he sank down onto his unmade bed and ran a clammy hand through his hair. It was pitiful. Aside from a psychotic, thirty-year-old nymphomaniac who was destroying his life, who actually *liked* him? Not Mike, obviously— although he'd probably get over it. Sam's lab partners were getting fed up with him, too. He'd been blowing them off since Christmas. And his girlfriend? They barely even spoke. If he didn't officially end things with Heather soon, it would probably be only a matter of time before *she* dumped *him*.

That left Gaia.

Right. After tonight Gaia probably wouldn't want to have anything to do with him, either. Of course she wouldn't. He'd left her in the park—where she'd been attacked—then dumped her unceremoniously on her front stoop after she'd keeled over. A hell of a dinner, wasn't it?

His eyes flashed to the phone. Maybe he should just call her. Maybe *she* had been the one who was calling and calling all night. It was possible, wasn't it? Yeah, right. It was also possible that the queen of England was calling, too. He knew damn well who it had been. The psycho. The foster mom. He couldn't bring himself even to *think* her name. And if he called that house, chances were very good that *she* would answer the phone.

So. Once again he found himself back where he started. Ground zero. Having confessed nothing. In the same state of panic. At this rate he was going to have an ulcer before he turned twenty-one. For all he knew, Ella had already told Gaia everything. Maybe she'd found Heather and told *her*, too. Anything could happen.

But that wasn't what terrified him the most.

No . . . what terrified him the most was that a part of him—a subconscious part, buried deep within the darkest reaches of his psyche—might want that to happen. A part of him might secretly long for Ella to tell Gaia the truth. Because in a way, that would let Sam off the hook. And wasn't that what every coward wanted? Why else had he rushed Gaia back to her house tonight before she even woke up? He didn't want to deal with the truth. The truth was far too ugly.

And tomorrow he'd start over. Once again he'd go back to Gaia's house and keep a vigil outside her door until he caught her alone. Because there was always a chance that he'd miss her, or almost be hit by a car, or Gaia would be attacked . . . or some extraordinary set of circumstances would let him off the hook one more time.

After all, that subconscious strategy had worked pretty well so far.

ELLA'S CALL DIDN'T COME UNTIL

almost five o'clock in the morning. Not that this was any surprise. Nothing about the evening had been a surprise. In a way, that was what had been most

Bravo!

disheartening about the entire exercise: its utter predictability.

"Yes?" Loki answered languidly, staring out his window at the twinkling lights of Manhattan. Soon the sun would be coming up. He sighed. Another sleepless night. He hated trying to get to sleep at dawn. It was almost always impossible.

"Nothing to report," Ella stated. "I followed her to the park. She returned home afterward. She's in bed now—"

"You're lying," Loki interrupted. His tone betrayed his exhaustion, but little else. The simple fact of the matter was that he simply didn't care enough to feel *anything* toward this woman anymore.

"No, I'm not," Ella retorted. She actually had the audacity to sound indignant. He had to hand it to her: Ella was always sure of herself, of her own clear conscience. Even in the face of what she had done. Even in the face of the test she had so miserably failed. "I just went up to her room. She's there. In bed."

Loki snorted. "Interesting. So you're calling me from the house?"

"Of *course* not. I'm on the corner of Perry and Bleecker—"

"That's enough." Loki groaned. "So your report is that you followed Gaia to the park, then home. You don't want to add anything?"

After a brief pause Ella cleared her throat. "I . . . I went out for a while afterward. For a few drinks. That's why I'm calling so late."

"With George?" Loki asked, even though he knew full well that she hadn't seen her husband since six o'clock.

"Yes," Ella answered. "*You're* the one who's always telling me to spend more time with him. I figured a night on the town would do us some good."

Loki laughed. He almost felt like applauding. *Bravo!* He was beginning to remember why he'd hired Ella in the first place. In addition to being supremely confident, she was also an excellent actress. The two qualities went hand in hand. Outwardly, she still had the makings of a good agent. Too bad she'd lost control.

"What's so funny?" Ella demanded. She sounded like a five-year-old.

Loki sighed again. It was time to end this game. "What's funny is that you abandoned Gaia somewhere on Broadway and spent the rest of the night hounding the occupant of an NYU dormitory. Are you having an affair with a college professor?"

For maybe the first time since he'd known her, Ella didn't have an answer. She was speechless. Just as he'd known she would be.

"You don't have to answer that question," Loki continued. "I respect your privacy. But it might interest you to know that Gaia was attacked in the park tonight."

"What?" Ella gasped, unable to mask the terror in her voice.

You're right to be afraid, Loki thought. *I gave you one final opportunity to redeem yourself, and you let me down. There are no second chances.*

"Bu-But she's fine," Ella stammered. "I just saw her—"

"I know she's fine," Loki interrupted, smiling. "I know everything, remember?"

Again he heard nothing. Not even a breath. But that silence betrayed a terror far greater than any words could express.

"Ella, at its most basic level your assignment consists of only two tasks. The first is to monitor Gaia. The second is to keep her out of danger. You have repeatedly failed at both. Worse, you have repeatedly lied to me. This is no good."

"I'm sorry," she whispered. Her voice rose. "I won't let it happen again. I swear to you. It's just the pressure. Of living with George. Of everything." The words tumbled from her mouth in a panicked rush. "And I'm not having an affair. I just—"

"I don't care, Ella," he stated, cutting her off.

"But—"

He clicked off the phone. Once again his gaze swept over the Manhattan skyline. The situation was unfortunate. He'd invested so much energy in Ella, so much trust. And she *had* served him extremely well— up to a point. But he couldn't afford the luxury of second guessing his associates. Not anymore. Time was far too short. He knew what he had to do.

He had to take charge of monitoring Gaia himself.

TOM WATCHED SILENTLY AS ELLA RAN

The Pressure

back down Perry Street and clattered up the stairs of her brownstone.

But it wasn't until he heard the door being bolted that he allowed the pent-up air to explode from his lungs.

My God. He felt sick. He crouched behind a parked car, shivering uncontrollably. No wonder George was miserable. Ella clearly wanted out of their relationship. Tom had heard only a scrap of her conversation, but it was enough: *"I won't let it happen again. I swear to you. It's just the pressure of—of everything. And I'm not having an affair . . ."*

A dozen questions festered in his mind as he crept back down Perry Street toward Bleecker. He knew that agency life could put a strain on marriages; divorces were common. But still, something in Ella's voice suggested that her problems weren't just marital. No. Something deeper was going on.

Tom rounded the corner and headed east on Bleecker, burying his face in his jacket collar to protect it from the icy wind. He knew he shouldn't jump to conclusions. And he shouldn't interfere. Despite the fact that George and Ella were watching Tom's daughter, their marriage was *their* business. Still, the last bit he'd heard was particularly troubling: the part where Ella claimed that she *wasn't* having an affair. If she were, that would account for all the peculiarities and unhappiness. Tom wouldn't be pleased, obviously— but at least he would understand the situation.

But this . . . this was just baffling.

He went over her enigmatic remarks again. And again. The more he thought about them, the less they made sense. Who was on the other end? Judging from her subservient tone and obvious fear, it almost seemed like she was talking to a superior of some kind—somebody who had great influence and control over her life. But Ella didn't have a boss. She was a freelance photographer. So . . . a gallery owner, maybe? Or a magazine editor? Somebody who knew about George but still wanted to have an affair with Ella—and maybe suspected she was involved with somebody else . . .

Forget it. Tom shook his head. Speculating would accomplish nothing. Worse, it would drive him crazy. No, if he was going to get to the bottom of this, he would simply have to watch Ella as closely as he watched Gaia. *And* Sam Moon.

Too bad he couldn't be in three places at once.

Again, Tom's thoughts returned to his old friend George. He trusted him. He believed in George's instincts and his judgment enough to entrust to him his precious daughter. He hoped he hadn't made a terrible error.

A couple of years ago, before the accident, my sister used to love showing me off to her hip, twenty-something Manhattan posse. "Do you guys know my brother, Ed? He's, like, the most killer skateboarder. He's gonna break a lot of hearts someday. Just look at him. Yes, sir. The Heartbreak Kid."

I always pretended to be really embarrassed, too—even though I loved the attention. It was awesome. I mean, having a bunch of hot twenty-two-year-old girls calling you the Heartbreak Kid? What fifteen-year-old boy *wouldn't* love that? And it got even better when I started going out with Heather. I became an official stud.

But then *ka-blammo!* Game over. Accident. Hospital. Paralysis. Wheelchair.

It was kind of hard to keep being a stud.

My sister couldn't deal. So she literally disappeared. I can count the number of times I've seen her since the accident on one hand. The first time was right afterward, and it was so forced and awkward I found myself trying to make *her* feel better. Since then it's always been with a group of her friends. As if they can offer some kind of protection. A buffer to keep her from seeing reality.

The real icing on the cake, though, is that she always says really painful and inappropriate things to them. And always in a very loud voice: "You'll be back on your feet in no time, Ed. Back to breaking girls' hearts. Just a couple of months more of rehabilitation, right?"

Wrong, sis. I'll be sitting here forever.

She has no idea she's making an ass of herself, though. She doesn't even know that she's pissing me off. For all I know, she might really believe what she's saying. In a way, she almost has to. Because then she doesn't have to deal with the very ugly truth: that the Heartbreak Kid is long gone. The Paraplegic Kid has taken his place.

She felt like she was *outside* herself. Completely detached. No **nightmare** longer in control. Somebody else was pulling the strings.

FIRST THING IN THE MORNING, GAIA

usually liked to sneak downstairs and stuff her face with some kind of sugar-coated cereal. Froot Loops were her personal favorite. She would pour a bowl and whorf it down before Ella and George

Dirty Bathwater

had a chance to wake up, then she would split for school. And if Ella and George happened to be up already, then Gaia would just have to walk straight out the door—and head to the nearest bodega for a rapid infusion of Krispy Kreme doughnuts.

Weekends were a little trickier.

She never knew what to expect. Sometimes Gaia would walk into the kitchen and find George there, hunched over the newspaper. Then she'd have to engage in actual conversation. Sometimes (very infrequently, thank God) George and Ella would make a lame attempt at a "family breakfast"—and Gaia would find herself subjected to French toast in the presence of the Nivens.

To put it bluntly, weekend mornings were a gamble.

But today Gaia was determined to avoid *any* contact with her foster parents. She'd set her alarm for seven o'clock, and—despite the struggle involved with forcing herself out of bed—she'd managed to get dressed by seven-twelve. She was on a mission. She was going to walk straight to Sam Moon's dorm room and find out what the hell had happened last night.

Yes. She was going to shake him out of bed and demand an answer to the following questions: (1) Why did he carry her home and drop her on the front stoop without any explanation? (2) *Did* he, in fact, carry her home and drop her on the front stoop without any explanation? (3) Why did he invite her out in the first place?

Sam owes me an explanation, she thought, tiptoeing down the stairs past Ella and George's room. Damn straight. At the very least he owed her an apology. She dashed down the last flight of stairs and yanked her coat from the closet, slamming the door behind her before she'd even pulled it on.

"Brrr," she muttered out loud.

It was another wintry day—clear and brisk. She quickly bundled up and headed toward the park, pulling her cap over her unkempt hair. But in spite of the freezing weather Gaia felt a strange optimism. A sense of control. She was finally going to get some answers. Besides, it was easy to feel in control when the streets were so quiet and deserted. Nothing unexpected could happen. Sam would be in his room, asleep. Just like everyone else.

She turned onto West Fourth Street and picked up her pace, jogging to keep warm. It was amazing how peaceful the park looked early on a Saturday morning. The trees and benches were bathed in the soft, golden glow of the dawn. And there were no freaks, no druggies . . . not even any homeless people. Only health nuts, in fact—people who were running or practicing t'ai chi. It was too cold for anyone else.

Gaia couldn't help but smirk. During these fleeting moments Washington Square Park could almost pass for a quaint little New England village square. *Almost.* In a way, the park was like a person: It wore many different faces, depending on the time of day.

As she crossed the street, she saw that a vendor was pushing his cart toward the northeast entrance—no doubt to intercept joggers coming to and from the NYU dorms. A couple of overweight, balding professor types were already close on his heels. Maybe she would stop for a quick doughnut on her way to Sam's. Yeah. She needed a sugar fix. She broke into a jog as she neared the chess tables. Sam wouldn't be getting up anytime before nine on a Saturday, anyhow.

"*Gaia.*"

The word was barely a whisper.

She wasn't even sure if she'd heard it. Her pace slowed.

"*Gaia.*"

There it was again. She frowned and glanced

behind her. She couldn't even tell where the voice had come from.

"Over here."

She turned toward the chess tables. . . .

At that moment her legs turned to jelly.

A man was sitting at one of the tables. A man with golden hair and piercing eyes, heavily bundled in black. A man who had seemed to materialize out of nowhere.

Her father.

He smiled at her.

No, no, no.

She staggered backward, breathless—as if she'd been struck in the face. This was impossible. A dream. Only seconds ago, that stone bench had been empty. She shook her head and blinked. In a moment she would wake up in the Nivens' house. Of course she would. She squeezed her eyes shut, then opened them.

But the vision remained.

It *was* a vision, wasn't it? Another hallucination, like that crazy flash she'd had when the car had hit her yesterday . . .

"It's okay, Gaia," he called, beckoning to her. "I know what you're thinking."

You know what I'm . . . okay. Definitely a dream. Verging on a nightmare. A spasm of heat shot through her. Her mind emptied—as if every thought and emotion were merely dust motes in a tubful of dirty bathwater, now rapidly swirling down a drain.

"I'm not your father," he said.

"Oh my God," she found herself whispering.

This *wasn't* a vision. No. It was her uncle. The same uncle she'd seen for that fleeting instant in the park that night so many months ago. The one who'd saved her life. Some of the tension began to melt away. Disjointed memories flashed through her head: her lying on the ground, staring up at his face . . . that old song from the seventies: "Rescue Me" . . . dancing with her mother and father as a little child. . . .

"Please, Gaia," he implored. "Come sit. I don't have much time."

Her feet began to shuffle toward him. She felt like she was *outside* herself. Completely detached. No longer in control. Somebody else was pulling the strings. Her uncle, perhaps. But certainly not *her.* Not Gaia Moore. Not the girl who had left the Nivens' brownstone only minutes ago to confront Sam Moon . . .

"That's it," her uncle murmured as she eased herself down on the bench across from him. "Yes. Just relax. It's so good to see you."

Gaia opened her mouth, but she couldn't speak. Maybe it was best just not to try. She stared at her uncle, drinking in every feature of his face: his piercing blue eyes, his rugged skin, the broad lips that were so much like her own. But for the first time she noticed subtle differences between him and her father. Her uncle's jaw was more square than her father's, more angular. It exuded greater strength, somehow. And power.

He smiled. "It's fitting that we're facing each other across a chessboard, don't you think? We both love the game."

How am I supposed to answer that? Gaia wondered. *How is it you know so much about me? I didn't even know you existed until this year. All I can think of when I look at you is my own father. . . .*

"It's fitting for another reason, too," he said gravely. "We live in a dangerous world. And time is short." He reached into his pocket and pulled out a small card, then slid it across the smooth checkerboard surface. He tapped it with a gloved finger. "This is my contact information. Use it anytime you feel the need."

Gaia glanced down at the card. Time slowed to a crawl. The universe shrank to this chess table, to this moment, to *them*. Part of her had been longing for such a meeting ever since her father had vanished. A member of her family was reaching out to her. A *real* member—someone who shared her blood . . . someone who could understand her in a way nobody else could. But her hands remained at her sides. She couldn't bring herself to take the card. Why? Because if she allowed herself the possibility of getting close to him, she might lose him? The way she lost everyone else?

"I know you've suffered," he said, as if reading her mind. "But know this, Gaia: I'm here for you. Remember when I saw you here the first time? I promised I wouldn't be far. I promised I'd come back for you. And here I am. I never break my promises, Gaia. Never."

I guess that's another difference between you and Dad, Gaia thought bitterly. She felt the wetness on her cheeks even before she realized she was crying. She sniffed and wiped her face with her coat sleeve, clenching her jaw. This was great. Way to make an impression. Now her uncle probably thought she was a blubbering little baby.

"I'll talk to you again soon, Gaia," he whispered. He reached over and patted her shoulder, then abruptly stood and hurried from the table.

"Wait!" Gaia called.

He paused and glanced over his shoulder.

"What—what's your *name?*" she stammered.

A smile crossed his face. "Oliver," he answered.

And with that, he turned—not walking, not running . . . but seemingly *gliding,* moving with an effortless economy of motion that astounded her. He vanished around the corner of Waverly Place in seconds.

Gaia exhaled deeply.

Her body quivered. Tears still flowed freely down her cheeks. Her eyes fell back to the card. A single ten-digit phone number was printed there, with no other information. That was it. This flimsy little thing was the only evidence that she'd even *seen* her uncle—that the mysterious encounter had even taken place. She shook her head and forced herself to take it.

Oliver. Oliver Moore, she supposed.

Why had he chosen to contact her in this way, by sneaking up on her on a Saturday morning in the park? Why hadn't he just called the Nivens? There must be a good reason . . . or *was* there? *"We live in a dangerous world,"* he'd said, *"and time is short."* The words were so vague. Almost *trite.* Yeah . . . now that she thought about it, they sounded like the kind of thing somebody would say in a grade-D action flick. He was obviously a smart guy, but he chose to speak to her in clichés. It wasn't exactly intimate family conversation. She couldn't help but get a little pissed. Was he trying to hint that *she* was in danger? And if so, why didn't he just come out and say it?

One thing was for certain. She needed to be alone, to *think.* She was in no condition to talk to Sam Moon. No way. Taking a deep breath, she jumped up and ran from the park as fast as her legs would carry her.

I'VE JUMPED THIS STAIRCASE A

thousand times. Get up some speed, hop up onto the railing—then whoosh . . . it's all gravy. This is gonna be a breeze.

Three of the Major Food Groups

But Heather's scared.

Heather's always scared. I can see her down there, way at the bottom. She looks so small. She's yelling something to me.

But I can't hear what it is. It doesn't matter, though. I gotta do this.

The skateboard feels good under my feet. I glance back down the staircase. It's much longer than it was before. And Heather isn't alone down there. No, Phoebe is with her, too. And so is my sister. And Gaia. They're all screaming at me.

"Don't do it, Ed! Don't do it. Ed! Ed!"

But it's too late. I'm already on my way—

Ed flinched. His eyelids popped open. He was gasping for breath.

Heather was standing over him, gently shaking his shoulder.

"Ed?" she whispered. "Ed? Are you okay?"

"Uh . . ." He blinked. His voice sounded like a frog's. He shook his head. *Jesus.* Gradually his breathing slowed. His surroundings began to take shape around him. He wasn't standing at the top of a forty-story staircase. No. He was *sitting*. In his wheelchair. In the hallway outside the emergency room of St. Vincent's Hospital.

Heather crouched beside him so their eyes were at the same level. Her face was creased with concern. "I think you were having a nightmare," she said.

"I guess," he croaked.

The dark fog of the dream lifted, melting away into the nothingness. Ed's shoulders slumped. He wouldn't have called it a nightmare. No. Because no matter how bad his dreams got—even if he was being chased by an ax-wielding maniac through a shark-filled swamp—he was always *upright*. He could run. He could walk. He could freaking *dance* if he wanted to. The wheelchair had no place in the enchanted world of Ed Fargo's subconscious. So, no, he didn't have nightmares. Only dreams—dreams that were like warm embraces, slipping away in an instant when he came back to the real world and leaving him in solitude.

"You're sure you're all right?" Heather asked.

He nodded quickly, forcing himself to smile. He refused to let his usual morning grouchiness intrude here. He was the last person Heather should be worrying about. "Any word on Phoebe?" he asked.

"Yeah, actually, the doctor says she's really improving,"

Heather said with false cheerfulness. She stood up straight. "They upgraded her condition from critical to stable. Soon they're gonna move her out of intensive care and into a different wing." Her voice sounded strained, high-pitched. "The biggest problem was the dehydration, so they've been flooding her body with fluids. . . ." She trailed off.

"Can we go in and see her?" Ed asked.

Heather shook her head. "Not until later."

"Oh. Okay." He chewed his lip and glanced at the vinyl couch. "Where's your mom?"

"She went home." Heather managed a shaky grin and shrugged. She had obviously been crying. Recently. Her eyes were red and puffy, and she'd scrubbed all the makeup off her face. Her skin looked dry, colorless. "Which I take as a good sign. She wouldn't have left if she was really worried. So things are looking up."

Nice try, Heather, Ed thought sadly. Maybe if she said those words out loud, she would start to believe them herself. She deserved to believe them. Any comfort was enough.

Heather drew in a sharp breath. "Look, Ed . . . I want to tell you, I really think it's amazing what you're doing."

"What?" he asked nonchalantly. "Sleeping in a wheelchair? It's nothing. I do it all the time."

"No . . . *you* know. . . . Oh, Jesus." She shook her

head and laughed. "Why do you always make a joke out of everything?"

He shrugged. "Hey, I make people laugh, don't I?"

"Yeah." She looked down at him, her face softening. "Yeah, you do."

Ed stared up at her.

She held his gaze. Neither of them moved. Neither of them even blinked. He swallowed. It had been so long since he'd looked into her eyes like this—just *looked*, without saying anything . . . without *having* to say anything. But he knew the moment couldn't last forever. And the longer he prolonged it, the more he would torture himself with memories of the past. *Their* past. He turned away toward the candy machine.

"You know, I'm kind of hungry," he remarked. "A rousing breakfast of potato chips and chocolate sounds like just the thing."

He released the brakes on his chair, but Heather planted herself firmly in front of him, blocking his path.

"No way," she said with a smirk.

Ed cocked his eyebrow. "No way *what?*"

"No way am I going to let you eat potato chips and chocolate for breakfast."

"Oh, no?" He had to laugh. "Why? Are you concerned about my health? Let me tell you, Heather— potato chips get a really bad rap. They actually contain three of the major food groups. The grease group, the salt group, and the fat group—"

"I don't give a shit about your health, Ed," Heather interrupted, grinning tiredly. "I just want to take you out for breakfast. Okay?"

He sighed. "You don't have to do that."

"I know I don't," she stated. "But I'm going to do it, anyway."

Ed smiled. "Now, that's the Heather Gannis I know and love. The one who won't take no for an answer."

"You got that right. Let's go." She stepped aside and waved toward the exit with a flourish, as if she'd just laid out a red carpet. "And don't worry. I'll make sure you get plenty of grease, salt, and fat."

AFTER WANDERING THE STREETS

aimlessly for a few hours, Gaia looked up to find herself standing right outside Ed's building on First Avenue.

Don't Ask, Don't Tell

Not a big shocker. She kind of knew she'd end up here. Her feet just seemed to be naturally drawn toward the place—like a couple of moths toward a big lightbulb. Besides, she was freezing cold. She could stand to be inside for a while. Her nose was completely numb. And she didn't exactly relish the thought of going back to Ella Central. Or sitting alone in a coffee shop.

No. Right now the "alone" part of her life was starting to wear pretty thin.

The fact of the matter was that the more she walked around, going over what had happened with her uncle . . . *Oliver*, again and again, the more she started to get creeped out. She wasn't *scared*, obviously. She was just . . . confused. The whole exchange had been so *weird*.

Gaia glanced at the building's glass double doors, rubbing her sides with her arms for warmth, debating whether or not to buzz Ed's apartment. He was probably up, wasn't he? Yeah. It was almost ten. Anyway, this was kind of an emergency. For starters, she needed to apologize to him in person for blowing him off last night. And more important—*much* more important—she needed to spill her guts about her uncle.

Strange how things change, isn't it?

She shook her head as she walked up to the buzzer. Here she was, going to *confide* in someone. *Her.* Gaia Moore. The girl with an armor of secrets as thick as the Great Wall of China. Until very recently her and Ed's friendship had been defined by a simple rule: Don't ask;

don't tell. Ed didn't ask her about her life, and she didn't tell him about it. And the coolest part of this rule (or so Gaia once thought) was that neither of them ever had to acknowledge it. It was unspoken. Understood.

But after Mary died, the rule changed.

It was Ed's doing, of course. Gaia had resisted the change as stubbornly as she could—nearly killing herself and Ed in the process. But after an initial bout of pain she realized that she *had* to talk about *some* things. With *somebody*. If she didn't, she would simply explode. Or go insane. Or worse.

She pressed the button for the Fargos' apartment.

A few seconds later there was a burst of static.

"Hello?" Mrs. Fargo answered.

"Um . . . hi," Gaia said awkwardly. "It's Gaia Moore, Ed's friend. I was just in the neighborhood, and I was wondering if Ed was home." *Good Lord.* Did that sound as lame as she thought it did?

"No, he's not, Gaia," Mrs. Fargo answered. She sounded harried, as if she were in a rush. "He spent the night at Heather's."

Gaia stiffened. Her heart bounced in her chest. She must not have heard the woman correctly. "Excuse me? Did you say Heather's?"

"That's right. Heather Gannis. She's having some kind of crisis. Listen, I'm sorry, dear, but we're in the middle of something. I'll tell Ed you stopped by. You might try reaching him at the Gannises, though. Good-bye."

That was it.

Conversation over. Gaia blinked. She stared at the buzzer through the tendrils of her frozen breath. Her heart pounded. Ed. At Heather's. Impossible. The universe had flipped over and turned itself inside out. This wasn't planet Earth. This was some bizarro, alternate planet. One where long-lost uncles jumped out and said, "Boo!" One where Ed's parents let him spend the night at his ex-girlfriend's house. One where Ed *wanted* to spend the night at his ex-girlfriend's house. What kind of crisis could Heather be *having*, anyway? She was too shallow to have a crisis. Did she misplace her lip gloss or something?

Gaia suddenly realized she was grinding her teeth. And clenching her fists at her sides. Whatever. There was no point in getting angry. This obviously wasn't the optimum moment to pick for confiding.

Monkey Suit City

"SO I CAN REALLY ORDER WHATEVER I want?" Ed asked tentatively from behind his menu. "Everything here looks so expensive...."

"Sky's the limit," Heather answered, leaning back in her chair. She'd picked The Half

Moon on purpose—not only because it was down the block from the hospital, but precisely because it *was* so expensive. She'd read about the place in a very pretentious article in *New York* magazine a week or so ago. She remembered it word for word, in fact: "A hipper-than-thou twenty-four-hour diner in the new retro style: midcentury meets the millennium." Whatever that meant. As far as Heather could tell, this place looked just like any other diner—except for all the hair gel and cell phones.

Of course, another crucial difference was that a serving of pancakes cost twenty dollars. But Heather wanted Ed to feel pampered. He'd earned it.

"I . . . uh, think I'm just going to have a fried egg sandwich," he mumbled. He closed the menu and put it down.

Heather frowned at him. "Are you *sure?*"

"Yeah. I figure an egg sandwich with lots of ketchup is the grossest thing I could possibly eat." He glanced around the restaurant. "I want to see how the crowd reacts."

They'll probably ask you to leave, Heather thought, grinning ruefully. She already *had* noticed a couple of disapproving glances as they'd come in. Not that it was any big surprise. It was a miracle they'd even been seated. They both looked like derelicts—unbathed and unkempt. But a few customers had the gall to stare at Ed's wheelchair, as if being disabled was somehow offensive. Uncouth. Gauche. Why was it that members of "polite society" were always the most rude? Actually, that wasn't a tough one to answer. It was because people were goddamn hypocrites.

"You know, it's a good thing you brought me here," Ed said, rolling his eyes. "This'll be good training for tomorrow."

Heather blinked at him. "What's tomorrow?"

"My sister's engagement party." He groaned.

"Oh, that's *right*." In all the miserable insanity of the past eighteen hours, she'd completely forgotten about Victoria. But she was secretly relieved Ed had brought it up. It meant they could talk about something other than Phoebe—at least for a while. "So where's it gonna be?"

Ed bowed his head. "You're not gonna believe this," he muttered. "The Plaza Hotel."

Heather's eyes widened. "Are you serious?" she whispered. *Jeez.* Victoria's fiancé must be loaded. There was no way the Fargos would ever throw a party at the Plaza. That was not their style.

"Unfortunately, I am." He sighed and slumped back in his chair. "It's gonna suck so bad. I mean, it's black tie and everything. Monkey suit city."

"Really?" She couldn't help but smile. The thought of Ed's being all decked out in a tuxedo was kind of . . . well, cute.

Ed frowned. "What?"

135

"I don't know," she remarked casually. "It might not be so bad."

"Believe me, it is." He shook his head. "I mean, it's not just the fact that I'm gonna be surrounded by a bunch of multibillionaires. It's also that I won't know a single person . . . except my parents and my sister and a few of my sister's friends—and all of them have a habit of saying really lame, stilted things that make me feel like crap. And what makes it even worse is that my mom said I could invite somebody, and I was going to—" He abruptly broke off in midsentence.

Heather stared at him. "What?"

"Nothing. It's just . . ." He lowered his eyes. His face turned slightly pinkish.

Hmmm. A thought dawned on Heather. Ed was embarrassed about something. Something that had just popped out of his mouth. Something having to do with her, obviously. And that probably meant that he had planned on asking *her* to go with him. But after last night, after Phoebe, he *couldn't* ask her. Or so he thought.

"Ed, were you going to ask me to go?" she asked him, point-blank.

His head popped up. "No!" he exclaimed. "I mean, no—what I mean to say is . . . I just . . . Forget it." His face was now beet red. He buried it in his hands.

"Because I'd be honored to go," she murmured.

He froze. His arms fell to the table with a clumsy

136

thud. He gaped at her as if she'd just offered to commit some horrible crime. "You *would?*"

She laughed. "Sure. It would give me a chance to wear that black strapless thing you once loved so well," she said breezily, suggestively.

The words didn't seem to register. "But . . . but what about . . ."

"Phoebe?" she finished. She leaned across the table. "Phoebe's not going to die, but her progress is going to be really slow. She's not going to be all better anytime soon. Probably years. I'm going to do everything I can for her, but I'm not going to stop living my life in the meantime. Nobody's going to fix Phoebe but Phoebe."

Slowly his face began to return to its normal color. He nodded. But he still seemed hesitant.

"It's *okay,* Ed," she insisted. "Besides, I love the grand ballroom of the Plaza Hotel. I'll take any excuse."

He laughed. "Well, in that case . . ."

"Good. It's settled." She grinned at him, suddenly feeling very content. It was a good thing she was able to play the whole thing off so smoothly. Because the truth of the matter was that this party could have been in the back of some bar in Penn Station, and she still would have agreed to go.

As long as she could be with Ed Fargo.

Strange how fate works, isn't it?

I mean, there I was, totally freaking out, on the verge of having to admit to Heather that I was planning on asking Gaia out on a date (although technically this engagement party thing is *not* a date)—which, needless to say, would have ruined all those warm, fuzzy feelings that have built up between my ex and me during the past twenty-four hours.

That's not an exaggeration, either. Our newfound friendship would have gone up in smoke. Poof. Just like that. See, I know Heather. And if there's one thing she can't stand, it's knowing that somebody else may be more desirable than her. Particularly if that person is named Gaia Moore. You might say Gaia is Heather's Achilles' heel. We all have one. (Mine is Gaia, too, by the way, in case you haven't guessed, but in a different way:

the way that turns me into a
slobbering dog whenever she's
around.)

Anyway, Heather probably would
have stormed out of the restaurant if I'd told her the truth.
She probably would have forbidden
me to visit Phoebe anymore.
That's how much she hates Gaia. I
mean, just look at the way she
acted last night. The mere fact
that I wanted to *call* Gaia pissed
her off. Majorly.

But luckily everything worked
out. Heather (in that typically
Heather-esque way) naturally
assumed that I wanted to take *her*
to the party. Of course. So she
took care of my dilemma for me.

And theoretically, this is
really the best-possible solu-
tion. Really. For one thing, Gaia
probably wouldn't want to go,
anyway. If she didn't want to
meet me at Blockbuster, chances
are pretty good she wouldn't want
to get dolled up to go to the
Plaza with me, either. For all I

know, she doesn't even own a dress. Come on, Gaia Moore in a dress? I guess she did wear some kind of skirt thing to Mary's funeral. But I almost have an easier time imagining Mike Tyson in a tutu than Gaia in one of those shiny, puffy outfits that girls wear to formal parties.

Heather *definitely* owns a dress, though. A bunch.

That also means I get to go to this party with a really hot date. Not to mention the fact that my sister *loves* Heather. So do my parents. So do all my sister's friends.

Best of all, I'll have somebody to talk to, somebody who can help me rag on all the lame-ass people who are going to be there.

It's really perfect this way. Really.

So why do I feel like shit?

Every track
was covered,
every alibi in
place; she'd
constructed a
devious
network of
lies that was
impossible to
crack.

a
bad
first

"I'LL SEE YOU IN A LITTLE WHILE,

honey," Ella called, slipping into her coat. "I'm just running over to Mercer Street to drop off some negatives—"

"Come here," George interrupted from the living room.

She paused. The muscles in her stomach clenched. George actually sounded *annoyed*. Wonderful. This was

The Difference Between Betrayal and Sadism

just what she needed. A little marital spat, just to keep things lively. She could feel rage creeping up on her like a rising tide, but she forced herself to take three quick breaths. "I'm kind of in a rush," she answered as politely as she could manage.

"This is important," George insisted.

So is staying alive, Ella answered silently. She glanced at her watch. It was nearly three o'clock. Rage shifted to nervousness . . . then fear. She had to report to Loki at three-thirty. Sharp. After last night's debacle she couldn't afford another screwup. She couldn't even afford the most remote *possibility* of a screwup. Her life depended on it. She wasn't an idiot.

"I'm sorry, George, but—"

"Come *here*, dammit!" he barked.

Ella froze, suddenly petrified with shock.

My God. This was a first. A bad first. In all the time she'd known George, he'd never once raised his voice with her. Her heart began to race. There was no way he could suspect her true identity. Was there? She'd been careful that every track was covered, every alibi in place; she'd constructed a devious network of lies. Granted, she'd allowed herself a few moments of recklessness recently, but George adored her. He would never suspect . . .

She stepped into the living room.

The curtains were drawn. The room was completely dark, in fact—except for the light of a roaring fire. George was slumped on the leather couch, staring at the fireplace. His face was twisted in a sour grimace, his craggy features grotesque in the flickering orange light. A nearly empty bottle of chardonnay sat on the mahogany coffee table. An empty glass sat beside it. Ella swallowed. George never drank this early in the day.

"What's wrong?" she murmured.

He shook his head. "That's not the question," he said, his gaze fixed on the fire. "The question is, what's *right?*"

Ella's heart was thumping so loudly and painfully now that she worried he might hear it over the crackling flames. "What do you mean?"

"Just look at us, Ella," he stated. "I mean, really *look* at us. When was the last time we talked? When was the last time we even said *hello?*"

"I . . . It's just—I've been busy," she stammered. Her eyes flitted down to her watch. Time was slipping away. It would take her twenty minutes to get uptown—even if there was no traffic. She continued to speak, but her brain was on autopilot. "The beginning of the year is always the time when galleries look for new artists, so it's important that I show my work to as many people as possible—"

"What time did you get in last night?" he demanded, suddenly facing her.

She blinked. "I . . . uh . . . well, it was late." She smiled apologetically. "I went to a party in SoHo and lost track of the time."

He remained silent for a moment. His lips pressed into a tight line. His eyes were cold. "And who was at this party?" he finally whispered.

"Just, um, a couple of friends," she said. Her voice started to quaver. She couldn't help it. In spite of all her years of rigorous training, she could feel herself panicking. The helplessness was acute. At any moment her disguise might slip. She was certain of it. He'd never looked at her this way before . . . with such *venom*. At any moment he might be able to see her for who she really was.

"A boyfriend?" he growled.

Ella gaped at him. Was *that* what this was about? Did he think she was having an affair? She almost felt like laughing. All at once the fear fluttered away, and the perfectly crafted wall went up again. An affair! Ha! What a *relief*. Handling this would be no problem at all. This was *nothing*. And as she'd learned from Loki himself, suspicious accusations were best countered with anger.

"You think I have a boyfriend?" she snapped indignantly.

His face fell. "I . . . I don't know *what* to think," he muttered.

"George, has it ever occurred to you that I'm trying to get a career off the ground?" she asked. Confidence surged through her. *This* was the reward for serving Loki—to control this spineless pawn. The words flowed as if she were reading them from a page. "I don't accuse *you* of seeing a mistress when you disappear on your missions for weeks at a time. Marriage is about trust, George. It works both ways."

He turned back to the fire. "I know," he choked out, his voice breaking. "And I *do* trust you. I just want things to be . . . to be the way they were."

For the briefest instant Ella almost felt sorry for him. After all, he'd been living a lie—a lie that was tearing him apart, no less—and he didn't even know it.

Saddest of all, the lie would ultimately kill him. Quite soon, in fact.

But that was the price he knew he could pay when he chose his profession. One could never be too cautious. Even with those you loved. Even with those whom you believed loved you in return.

"Things will get better, George," she finally whispered. "I promise."

She bit her lip, then turned and hurried from the

room. It was best to leave the argument at that. There was no point in torturing George unnecessarily.

Even Ella could appreciate the difference between betrayal and sadism.

I'M NOT GOING TO PUT THIS OFF
any longer.

Sam shook his head, marching determinedly down Perry Street toward the Nivens' brownstone. Enough was enough. He was going to tell Gaia the truth. Now. Face-to-face. He didn't even care if Ella was home. He'd spill it all in front of her. What could she do? Deny it?

The Tell-tale Heart

Maybe her husband would be home, too. Fine. The more the merrier. After all, George Niven had a right to know what his wife was up to as well. Everybody did. The guilt was tearing Sam apart. It was simply too much to bear. What was that story by Edgar Allan Poe? *The Tell-tale Heart*. Right. It was about the heart of a murder victim that continued to beat after he'd been buried under some floorboards, driving his murderer to madness . . . until the murderer finally had to confess to his crime.

148

Only *this* time the tell-tale heart was beating inside Sam Moon—because Sam Moon was killing himself.

He paused in front of the stoop, taking a moment to collect himself.

The door creaked open.

Uh-oh. He winced.

It had to be Ella. Wearing that ridiculous coat. She didn't even seem to notice him. She trotted quickly down the steps, her head down. He stood there, frozen in place—an animal caught in headlights. She barreled right into him. He staggered backward, nearly falling on his back.

"*Excuse* me," she snapped. "Watch . . ." Her face suddenly brightened. She smiled. "Sam? I'm sorry. I didn't expect to see *you*."

He brushed himself off and stood up straight. It took a continuous effort of will not to leap forward and smash her in the face with his fist.

"What are you doing here?" she asked.

"What do you *think*," he hissed. "I'm looking for Gaia."

Ella frowned. "Oh. She's not here. But don't worry." Her smile reappeared. "Our secret is safe with us. Gaia doesn't know a thing."

"I don't believe you," he said in a hollow voice.

Ella laughed, then shook her head and began walking briskly toward West Fourth Street. "Suit yourself. Go ahead and check. She's not there."

Sam's eyes flashed to the door, then back to Ella's

retreating form. "I meant what I said," he called after her. "If you tell her anything . . ."

"I know, I know," she answered, sounding bored. She didn't even bother to look over her shoulder. "You'll kill me."

Anger engulfed him like a flash flood . . . then strangely, it vanished—leaving only numbness in its place. He watched blankly as Ella hailed a cab and sped off into the afternoon. There was nothing he could do, was there? This woman, this *lunatic*, was now part of his life. Forever. She was stronger than he was. Smarter. She had the upper hand. Even if he told Gaia the truth, what would that accomplish? He'd simply lose her for good. He'd destroy whatever slim chance they might have of ever being together.

But Ella would still be there. Ella would *always* be there.

TRAILING HIS DAUGHTER AROUND

downtown Manhattan was a useless exercise. Useless, frustrating, and agonizing. As the sun began to set, Tom finally decided to give up. Gaia was safe . . . at least for today.

Safe and alone.

A Shift in Focus

He'd never seen such isolation. At least not in anyone but himself. Apparently she had no close friends, the Moss girl having been the one exception. Sam Moon was a potential enemy of the most dire kind. There was also that boy in the wheelchair, but even *he* seemed to have disappeared.

Tom fought back tears as he watched Gaia stroll down Perry Street toward the Nivens' home. It was her face that tore him apart. Her face was a portrait of sadness. She hadn't smiled once all day. She hadn't even looked up from the grimy streets and sidewalks. He'd begun his surveillance at noon—she'd simply walked endlessly over the same territory, fists jammed in pockets, head down in the bitter cold.

That's how my daughter spends her Saturday. Roaming the city streets until night falls. A solitary figure.

He should have expected it, he supposed. Solitude ran in the family. All the Moores were cut off from the rest of humanity. Even his brother.

His breath quickened at the thought of his brother. From what he could deduce, Loki didn't intend to harm Gaia—at least not in the immediate future. On the contrary, if Loki was grooming her to join him, then he'd go out of his way to protect her.

So it was time to shift focus. It was time to concentrate his energies on potential threats: specifically Ella Niven and Sam Moon.

From: shred@alloymail.com
To: gaia13@alloymail.com
Time: 5:35 P.M.
Re: Car crashes, etc.

Hey, G$—

Wow. Hit by a car, huh? That's a story you can tell your grandkids. Apology accepted. No, I don't hate you. Don't sweat the missed connection. But write back or give me a call to let me know you're okay, all right? Maybe we can still watch that movie. I'm not doing anything tonight. I was thinking about renting *The Great Gatsby*. That way we don't have to read the book. What do you think?

—Ed

From: gaia13@alloymail.com
To: shred@alloymail.com
Time: 7:02 P.M.
Re: [No subject]
    I'd rather read the book.

Things I Hate About Heather Gannis:

1. She's beautiful, stylish, and sexy—in that really heinous New York City way.
2. She's a total bitch.
3. No one seems to notice this but me.
4. I almost got her killed once, so she makes me feel guilty.
5. She and Ed are suddenly best friends.
6. She invited Ed to spend the night at her house.
7. He accepted.
8. I have no idea *why* he accepted.
9. She seems to go out of her way to make my life hell, and she doesn't even know it.
10. And oh, yeah, I almost forgot—she's Sam's girlfriend.

It's strange how memory works. I can't remember much of the past five years—at least not specific details. All the assignments seem to blur together in an endless stream of plane flights and clandestine meetings, of shadowy figures and aliases and death. Even the cities blend together: Prague, São Paolo, Brazzaville, Tokyo. . . . The list is as long as it is depressing. I've been to every continent, and I can't tell any of them apart.

But I remember the day Gaia was born with such clarity that it frightens me. Every detail of the hospital waiting room is etched upon my mind: the stack of out-of-date *People* magazines, the threadbare orange carpeting, the buzzing fluorescent lights. I remember the nurses' smiles as I paced back and forth. The other two expectant fathers, sharing their anxiety with me. I remember wanting to hold Katia's hand so badly, I thought I would explode. But Katia's blood pressure had been spiking, putting her at risk, and they didn't want an excitable father in the OR.

And finally they called me in. Finally I was able to stand beside my Katia and gaze into my beautiful daughter's eyes.

I also remember thinking that something changed that day. Because until that day I thought that nobody else's eyes were as beautiful as my wife's. No other pair had that same capacity to captivate.

Not until Gaia came along.

Katia noticed the change, too. "Somebody stole your heart from me," she would joke during the first few years of Gaia's life.

"That's right," I would reply. "A beautiful blue-eyed blond."

Katia would always insist that Gaia's best features were from the Ukrainian side of the family: her strength, her beautiful skin, her intellect. And out of pride I

would deny it. I would insist
that she inherited her best qualities from me. I was half joking,
of course, but part of me was
serious. Gaia was so special that
I wanted to claim her as my own
creation.

I know now that Katia was
right. Gaia has more of her
mother inside her than she'll
ever know.

But I shouldn't dwell on the
past, even though my memories are
all that allow me to keep going.
I often think of the songs Katia
used to love—the old classic rock
and soul from the sixties and
seventies. American music made
her laugh out loud. Her eyes
would light up. She would dance.
It was so joyous, so unlike any
music she'd heard back home.

One line from one song in particular stands out.

*"I'd trade all of my tomorrows
for a single yesterday."*

Their bodies
were two
asteroids,
adrift in a
perfectly
space, **terrible**
caught
in each **time**
other's
gravitational
pull. . . .

ED'S MISERY EXISTED ON SEVERAL

levels.

At its most basic, he was uncomfortable. Physically. The ballroom was way too hot. The tuxedo, which his parents had bought for

Neobaroque— Cheesy

him for some unknown reason before his accident, didn't fit anymore. His pants were too short. They were chafing him at the waist. They barely cleared his knees. (At least he was prepared for a flood.) The shirt, jacket, and vest were also too small. The collar was like a freaking noose. Nobody seemed to remember that in the time he'd been confined to his wheelchair, his upper body had developed in order to compensate for his not being able to walk. But his parents told him he looked great. He could only imagine what Heather would think. (If she ever showed up. Where the hell *was* she, anyway?) If he twisted too far to the right or left, he might rip right out of his clothes, like the Incredible Hulk.

That could be funny, though. And this party definitely needed some comic relief. If you could call it a party.

It was amazing how you could put three hundred people in the same place and not tell any of them apart. Seriously. It wasn't just the monkey suits and gowns, either. Every male had slicked-back hair and perfect teeth, and every female was heavily made up and bone thin. Just looking at them reminded him of Phoebe, in fact—as if being here wasn't depressing enough. How many of *them* had eating disorders?

At least his parents had deserted him. Thank God. Ed usually liked to spend the hours from five to eight on a Sunday evening as far away from them as possible. It didn't matter *what* he was doing. He could be lying in a gutter. Fortunately, they had their hands full—what with maintaining their fake smiles and not bickering. Plus they were dealing with caterers, photographers, the band (a cheesy Frank Sinatra rip-off type thing), mindless chitchat. . . . It was going to be a hell of a night.

Then there was the place itself. A monument to human grossness. From his strategic spot, he had a perfect view of the decor. What would somebody call this style, exactly? Neobaroque-cheesy? Prepostmodern-garish? Everything was gold and maroon—gilded with little flowers and cherubs. All the furniture was covered in velvet. Ed had assumed that velvet had gone out of style during the seventies, but apparently it all just ended up here. Plus you couldn't move ten feet in any direction without catching a glimpse of yourself in a mirror. That made sense, though. Rich people were vain, and vain people liked to look at themselves. Blane sure as hell did. In the five minutes Ed had been here, Blane had already adjusted his goop-filled hair four times.

But Ed could deal with his future brother-in-law, the Plaza—even his ill-fitting tux. He'd *expected* all that. That wasn't the true root of his misery. No, the true root of his misery had nothing to do with the event itself.

It had to do with Gaia.

He swallowed, feeling queasy. Obviously she was mad at him for some reason. That e-mail had been . . . well, *curt*, to say the least. She hadn't even signed it G$. She'd used her real name. On purpose. To be stiff. Formal. Distant.

And Ed had absolutely no clue what he'd done.

Of course, he knew from long experience that there was no point in trying to figure out Gaia's bizarre mood swings. But at the very least he usually had some *clue* as to why she might be annoyed with him. Not this time, though. This was a total mystery.

The only possible reason he could think of was that Gaia had somehow found out that he was taking Heather to this party. His mom had mentioned that she'd stopped by the apartment . . . but he was pretty sure that was before he'd even *invited* Heather. Or rather, Heather had invited herself. And who would have told Gaia, anyway? Maybe his mom had said something about his hanging out with Heather. . . .

Whatever. Best to buck up. Maybe eat another of those shrimp things. Why ruin a perfectly terrible time?

AS THE TAXI PULLED INTO THE

Movie Star

circular driveway at the corner of Fifth Avenue and Central Park South, Heather couldn't help but feel a twinge of excitement. There was just something so undeniably *glamorous* about the moment. The Plaza looked like a giant, fairy-tale castle, with its little turrets and chimneys and flags.

A doorman in a top hat and shoulder epaulets rushed out and opened the door, offering a hand to help Heather slide out of the cab.

"Thank you," she murmured.

This must be what movie stars feel like, she thought, carefully lifting the hem of her black dress as she walked up the red-carpeted stairs. She had smiled to herself. She'd seen a bunch of actresses lifting their hems in the exact same way at last year's Oscars. She'd always secretly wanted to do it, too.

And now she was. It was funny: A dream of hers

had actually come true. How often did *that* happen in real life?

Thank you, Ed.

If the outside of the Plaza was impressive, though, the inside was awe inspiring. Heather tried not to gape as she drifted through the revolving door. Everybody was dressed in designer clothing. *Everybody.* The walls were lined with hand-painted murals and jewelry-box-size boutiques selling cigars and watches and expensive imported lingerie. She found herself eyeing the crowd for any celebrities. If there was anyplace in New York to spot a rock star or actor, this was it.

A sign near the grand staircase caught her attention.

FARGO-HARRISON ENGAGEMENT
5 P.M. TO 8 P.M.
MAIN BALLROOM

That's me, she thought dizzily. She headed quickly toward the ballroom's double doors, then paused under a vast, crystal chandelier. Maybe she should go to the ladies' room and freshen up a little bit. Yes. She was going to make an entrance. A *dramatic* entrance. She would dazzle Ed, knock his socks off. And not just at the start. She was going to make sure this evening was as magical for Ed as it was for her.

Transformed

thought with a snicker.

He'd parked his wheelchair at the edge of the dance floor for purposes of amusement, and he could see that it had been an excellent decision. His parents were out there, swinging up a storm. Or trying to. He didn't think he'd ever seen them dance before. Now he understood why. They looked like buffoons. His dad kept trying to lead his mother one way, but she kept trying to go another. They had absolutely no rhythm, either. But still, he had to hand it to them: Their smiles were still in place. A little strained, a little wary . . . but hanging on.

His sister and Blane, though—they were the real tragedy. Mom had mentioned that they were taking ballroom-dancing lessons, and it was very clear that they should have spent that money elsewhere. For one thing, Victoria was already clearly bombed. She must have started drinking at nine this morning. Otherwise she would *not* be trying to improvise with those disco moves. Blane was oblivious, though. He kept counting to himself out loud: "*One*-two, *three*-four . . ." Every time Victoria tried to wriggle free from his grip, he would glare at her.

These two were something, weren't they? A match made in heaven.

Incredibly enough, watching all the bullshit unfold was pretty enjoyable. Ed had thought he would miss not being able to dance, but for once in his life, he was thankful he had an excuse to sit out. The Sinatra wanna-be crooner was singing some song about how this chick wore her hat and sipped her drink and how they (who?) could never take the memory of that away from him . . . or something.

There was a delicate tap on his shoulder.

He glanced up—and nearly fell out of his wheelchair.

Heather had arrived. No, that was a massive under-statement. Heather had *transformed*. She was hardly recognizable. Her long, shiny dark hair was parted in the middle, cascading over her bare shoulders. She was wearing a sleeveless black gown that hugged every curve of her body. . . . It was almost as if she wasn't wearing *anything*, as if she'd simply been dipped in a vat of black ink from the chest down. It was actually a lot like the dress his sister was wearing, only on Heather it actually looked *good*. Best of all, she was the only female in the room whose makeup didn't look clownish and overdone.

"Well, aren't you going to say hello?" Heather asked, cocking her eyebrow.

"Oh—sorry, hey," he mumbled, trying not to stare at her. If he'd been hot before, he was practically sweating now. He glanced around the dance floor and gestured awkwardly. "So, welcome to the lamest party ever. You can thank me later."

She grinned down at him. "Oh, I don't know. It doesn't seem so bad."

"Uh . . . you didn't take drugs before you came here, did you?" he asked sarcastically.

"Very funny." She laughed and gave him a playful swat on the shoulder. "I just think it's kind of neat when people dress up really nicely. It's a change, you know?"

He shrugged. Actually, she might just have a point. He stole another quick peek at her hips as she swayed in time to the music. Heather's look was certainly a change. He wouldn't have imagined it possible that she could make herself even *more* beautiful than normal. But that was Heather. A constant kaleidoscope of surprise. It was weird. Sitting here in this bizarre ballroom, he almost felt like he was looking at her with fresh eyes. As if they'd never even met before. He could almost pretend there was no baggage, no history, just a clean slate—

Stop it.

Ed's face suddenly darkened. He wouldn't allow himself to fantasize, to live in a dream world. The setting might be highly surreal, but the reality remained unchanged. Heather was his ex-girlfriend. Far more important, Heather supposedly had a boyfriend. Besides, she'd hurt him too much in the past. Nothing could heal that. And unfortunately, his heart belonged to someone else. Pathetically enough, that someone else was probably even less attainable than Heather.

"Cheer up, Ed," Heather teased. "You might just have to go through something like this yourself someday."

"Yeah, right," he grumbled.

She flashed him another smile. "You look great, by the way," she remarked.

He swallowed. He was definitely sweating now. No doubt about it. He could feel the dampness on his stupid dress shirt. By the end of the night he'd probably look like he'd gotten into a shower, fully clothed.

"Thanks," he finally muttered. "So do you." He turned away, then glanced back up at her again. She hadn't looked away. She was still smiling at him. Still staring at him. And this time he couldn't break from *her* gaze, either—

"Oh my *God!*" a high-pitched voice shrieked, shattering the moment. "Heather Gannis? Is that *you?*"

Victoria. Ed hung his head. He could hear Victoria's heels clattering on the dance floor as she ran over to them. Wonderful. He'd known this was going to happen. He was kind of amazed it had taken her *this* long to embarrass him. His eyes flashed back to Heather. She was still looking at him but in a knowing, conspiratorial kind of way. He had to smile. Heather could relate. She, too, knew about Victoria's behavior.

"Wow!" Victoria exclaimed.

She teetered in front of Ed, staring Heather up and down, then reached out and snagged a champagne flute from a passing waiter. A couple of drops spilled on Ed's pants. She didn't notice, of course.

"Congratulations, Victoria," Heather said with a polite smile.

"Wow!" Victoria said again.

Ed frowned at her. Did Victoria leave her brain at home or something? Her vocabulary seemed to shrink in inverse proportion to the amount of booze she'd had.

Heather awkwardly cleared her throat. "So, um, this is really an amazing—"

"You're like, this . . . this *woman!*" Victoria interrupted. Her words were slurred. "I mean, look at you! The Heather I remember was a little girl."

Please go away, Ed thought, cringing. He knew his face was beet red. Not only was Victoria making an ass of herself, embarrassing Ed, and humiliating Heather—she was also talking loud enough to be heard in New Jersey.

"Thanks, Victoria," Heather mumbled.

"You still got it, Ed," Victoria announced. She clapped him on the shoulder, a little *too* hard. "You still got the touch. And once you're on your feet again . . . whew. Watch out, ladies! Stud on the loose!"

Victoria continued to jabber drunkenly, but Ed no longer heard a word she said. Blood pounded in his ears. He clutched at his armrests so violently, he was worried he would tear them right off. Why couldn't she just shut up and leave them alone? How could she stand to be so awful? So completely blind to reality? Maybe that's why she drank like a rock star. To hide from herself.

". . . you guys make the cutest couple, too—"

All at once his wheelchair jerked backward.

Whoa. He glanced up. Heather had taken the handles and was steering him toward the exit. A phony smile was plastered on her face. Her eyes were smoldering.

"Hey!" Victoria cried. "Where're ya goin'?"

"Oh, I'm sorry!" Heather called over her shoulder. "I just remembered, there was something in the lobby I wanted to show Ed. We'll come find you later, okay?" She leaned down by his ear. *"Not,"* she whispered.

Ed leaned back in his chair as they sped through the crowd. That was another great thing about Heather. She was a very fast thinker. Normally Ed hated it when somebody pushed him. Right now, however, he felt he was in good hands.

Attack of the Trustafarian Losers

being the lamest party ever. Victoria was certainly the lamest fiancée ever.

Heather peered down at Ed. At least he seemed to have recovered.

She had to say we made a cute couple, Heather thought, deftly maneuvering him down a narrow and relatively empty corridor, away from the lobby. She had to ruin what might have been a salvageable evening. It was astounding, really. Nobody was *that* socially retarded. Well, not unless they'd had eighty glasses of champagne.

Ed's wheelchair glided silently on the plush maroon carpeting. Heather picked up her pace as she rounded a corner. Her grip tightened around the handles. The plastic dug into her skin. To think that she'd actually felt *lucky* to be here—

"Um, Heather?" Ed murmured, glancing over his shoulder. "I think the speed limit in the Plaza is sixty-five miles an hour. At least, that's what it is in the rest of New York State."

"Oh, jeez," Heather mumbled apologetically. She stopped short. Bad idea. Ed grabbed at the armrests

173

to keep from tumbling onto the floor. "Whoops!" She blushed. "God, I'm sorry . . ."

"Don't sweat it," Ed said with a weary grin. He grabbed the wheels and spun himself around so that he was facing her. "I just prefer to be in control of my own wheels. It's a guy thing, you know."

Heather stared at him. Much to her surprise, she found herself bursting into laughter. It wasn't even that funny. It was more that she could finally *relax*. Ed was incredible that way. He always managed to shrug off any tension with a wisecrack. Then again, maybe she was just laughing because he looked so cute. His hair was all rumpled, and his tie was crooked. His face was flushed and sweaty.

Ed glanced around the hallway, frowning. "Where are we, anyway?"

"Good question," Heather muttered. She really didn't care, though. Wherever it was, it was secluded. Maybe it was a service route or something. The wallpaper seemed faded, and there were no mirrors or boutiques. There was a pair of thick double doors at the end of the hallway. Guests probably weren't supposed to be in here. Which was fine with her. It meant that they were safe from Victoria.

"So," Ed said, sighing. "Thanks for getting me out of there."

Heather raised her eyebrows. "I was getting us *both* out of there."

Ed looked up at her. A smile spread across his face. Before she knew it, they were both cracking up. It was that or get pissed off.

Finally she took a deep breath. She shook her head. "You know what's really pathetic?" she asked.

"That we have to hide?" Ed suggested.

"Well, yes—but that's not it. It's just . . . Victoria and her pals are supposed to represent, like, the crème de la crème, you know? And it just seems—well, it seems like they're all a bunch of morons. They're not classy or anything. They're just these spoiled . . . brats."

Ed furrowed his brow in mock surprise. "Wait a minute. Am I hearing what I think I'm hearing? Is Heather Gannis dissing the wealthy, empty-headed, and fashionable? Is she dissing everything she once aspired to be?"

"Ha ha ha," she said dryly. "I'll have you know—"

"Shhh!" Ed suddenly interrupted. He put a finger over his mouth and sat up straight, peering behind her.

The sound of a few drunken giggles drifted around the corner from the direction of the lobby.

". . . what do you think's down here?" somebody was asking.

Uh-oh. Heather exchanged a petrified glance with Ed.

"We gotta hide!" he hissed.

Heather's eyes flashed to the set of double doors. "Maybe those are open," she said. She ran past him, nearly tripping on her dress. The latch jiggled when she grabbed it. Good sign. With a violent yank she pulled open the door. Hallelujah! She glanced back at Ed. He was already close on her heels. The giggles grew louder. Heather couldn't help but laugh, too. It was like some absurd horror movie: *Attack of the Trustafarian Losers.* She held open the door for Ed as he rolled through—then dashed in behind him.

The door swung shut. *Bam!*

"Uh . . . Heather?" Ed asked.

She didn't answer him. Because she knew what he was going to say.

It was pitch black in here.

"OOH," ED WHISPERED, GRINNING. "Spooky."

"Shut up, Ed." Heather groaned.

He laughed. Now *this* was comedy. They'd probably be trapped in this room forever (if it even

What's Everything?

was a room; it could be a garage, for all he knew). He blinked and squinted in an effort to see something— *anything*—but it was no use. He might as well have been blindfolded.

"I don't hear anything anymore," Heather whispered. Her voice sounded strangely echoey. Maybe they *were* in a garage. Or an auditorium. Or maybe they'd entered some sort of other dimension—which would be great because then he'd never have to see Victoria or Blane again. "Do you think they turned back?"

"Probably," Ed said dryly. "They probably get nervous if they get too far from the champagne and caviar."

Heather didn't say anything for a moment. He could hear her shuffling around blindly—first farther away, then closer. Suddenly she bumped right into his wheelchair.

"Ouch!" she whispered.

"Sorry," he mumbled.

They both laughed. Ed felt his wheelchair shift as she grabbed onto the back of it. She stood there, running her fingers over the seat, probably trying to orient herself. She shifted to the left.

"You know, I kind of like it in here," she said. He heard her dress swishing as she slowly sank on the floor beside him. "It's a part of the Plaza you never see," she added with a chuckle. "Get it?"

Ed rolled his eyes. "That sounds like the kind of joke my dad would make."

"Yeah, well, I guess wearing an evening gown makes me act like an adult," she remarked. "Lame humor and all."

"Too bad dressing up doesn't have the same effect on Victoria," Ed muttered.

Heather didn't reply. He could hear her breathing softly. The seconds ticked by, drawing out longer and longer. Ed shifted in his seat. The combination of utter darkness and near silence *was* a little creepy, actually. Maybe they should try to feel their way to the door.

"Ed, I'm sorry," Heather suddenly blurted out.

He grinned. "Hey, it wasn't your fault. We both wanted to get away—"

"No, no," she interrupted gently. "Not about coming in here. About ... everything."

Ed tensed. *Everything?* He didn't like the sound of that. He felt a prickling on the back of his neck, a dip in his stomach. There was a sadness in her tone—something he'd never heard before ... at least not until this weekend. He couldn't help but feel anxious. Part of him just wanted to bolt. Was she still talking about Victoria? Or was she talking about herself? About the past? About *their* past? He didn't know if he could deal with an apology for the past right now. It was too heavy, especially under these ridiculous circumstances. Besides, he didn't know if he was ready to *accept* an apology. There was too much to forgive.

But he heard himself asking the question, anyway. "What's everything?"

SOMEHOW IT WAS EASIER TALKING TO

Gravitational Pull

him when she couldn't see his face. Easier to apologize. Easier to confess.

Heather drew in a breath and bit her lip. If she didn't say this stuff right now, she knew she never would. Yes. This was the time—not only because of the way he'd been there for Phoebe, but because of the way Heather *hadn't* been there for him. For two whole years she'd wanted to ask for his absolution. To beg for it. And there was something about the darkness that encouraged risk... and intimacy. She felt like she could tell her secrets in the darkness. Back out in the light, her rational mind would take over and she would censor herself. She'd never get this chance again.

"I just wanted to say that I know I was a bitch to you," she whispered. Her voice was so strained that she felt like she was listening to somebody else speak. "I know it, and I *knew* it then, too—but I couldn't help it. It was easier to be a bitch."

Ed laughed grimly, but he didn't say anything.

"And I know you don't have to forgive me—"

"Good," he cut in, but his tone was soft. "Because I don't. Not for that."

Heather's throat tightened. She'd thought she'd been prepared for that, but she wasn't. Not at all. His rebuke stung like a slap. "It's just . . ."

"It's just that this chair has that effect on people," he finished for her. He sighed. "I know. You don't have to look any farther than my sister to figure that out."

"But it *shouldn't* have that effect on me," Heather insisted angrily. "I mean, I don't feel sorry for you. I don't feel pity for you. And you want to know why? Because *you* won't let me." Her voice grew hoarse. "I mean, I think that the very fact that you are considered disabled is actually *ironic*."

"Uh . . . you want to explain that one to me, Heather?"

"Because that label is *bullshit*," she spat. "It's bullshit if you or anyone else thinks that chair makes you less of a person. Because you're so much *more* of a person than anyone else I know. More than anyone else I've ever met. More open-minded, more thoughtful, more down-to-earth, more caring, more . . ." She shook her head, unable to finish—or even to organize her thoughts coherently. She didn't even know what she was *saying*. She was supposed to be delivering some kind of momentous apology, and here she was ranting in the blackness like a madwoman.

For a long time the two of them were silent.

Heather's lungs heaved. Her stomach was twisted into a dozen knots. But she was resolved not to regret what she'd said. No. She was *tired* of regret. She'd carried a sack of regret around with her for two goddamn years. The weight was unbearable. She had to let it go.

"Who are you, and what have you done with Heather Gannis?" Ed asked quietly.

Heather rolled her eyes. "Ed . . ."

"I'm serious," he stated. "I mean, there must be some kind of body snatcher in this place. Because the Heather Gannis I've observed for the last two years would never say something so sweet. Something so cool." His voice caught. "Something that actually makes me feel lucky. Which I thought was impossible."

Heather found herself reaching out for him even before she was fully aware of what she was doing. Tears filled her eyes for what must have been the hundredth time in forty-eight hours, but she didn't care anymore. She groped in the dark, motivated only by the desire to be as close to Ed as possible. Her fingers found his and intertwined with them. Those familiar fingers. So strong and tender. Her face swam blindly over the wheelchair. She was no longer in control. Forces beyond her understanding had taken over. Their bodies were two asteroids, adrift in space, caught in each other's gravitational pull. . . .

Her lips pressed against his, and the universe melted away.

I'm still not really sure what happened. All I know is, Victoria and Blane's engagement party did *not* turn out the way I expected.

I guess I should be thrilled. I mean, obviously I *am* thrilled. But the shock of it still hasn't worn off. The memory has this strange, dreamy feel—like it didn't really happen to me. It *couldn't* have happened to me.

I made out with Heather in a storage room in the Plaza Hotel.

It's almost funny. I mean, that's the kind of thing that happens in those lame teen movies that seem to come out every single week. "Boy in wheelchair gets hot chick! Now, *that's* Hollywood!" Even in my wildest fantasies, even when I used to daydream about getting back together with Heather *every single day,* I never thought I'd hook up with her like this. Every time I think of it, I want to throw up my arms and shout. Or break into a wild jig. (If I could.) I can't

sleep. I can't eat. I'm completely wound up.

Is that how love works,
though? I mean, do I just fall
head over heels for the last girl
I've kissed? Am I that pathetic?
Am I just your average, desperate, hard-up teenage guy with
haywire hormones? I guess so.
After all, those teen movies
don't lie. Besides, I fell head
over heels in love with Gaia
after we kissed during truth or
dare. Then again, I'd been head
over heels in love with her for a
while before that.

This was totally out of the
blue, though. Unexpected.
Magical.

I guess I shouldn't overthink
it. It just comes down to this:
Kissing Heather is the best feeling I've had in a long, long
time. And in a way, that's all
that matters.

But I can't help but feel
scared, either. It's not like
Heather hasn't let me down

before. I meant what I said: I'll never forgive her for what happened after the accident. In some ways, that hurt even more than the accident itself.

On the other hand, she isn't the same person she was then. Incredibly, my sister was absolutely right: Heather *was* a little girl back then. (Insert champagne breath and obnoxious laughter here.)

We've *both* changed, actually. Which makes me excited. Maybe we *can* make this work. Maybe I'll actually have a girlfriend again. A real girlfriend. Something I'd counted out. Something I'd resigned myself not to think about because I'd just assumed it was impossible.

And Heather wouldn't be just any girlfriend, either. No, she's an amazingly smart, amazingly sexy girl who knows me better than anyone. It's like I typed a program into a computer: "create ideal woman"—and out spat Heather.

Only . . . that's not the whole truth.

No. Because until this weekend, I didn't think my ideal woman was Heather at all. I thought it was Gaia. Then there's the unsavory matter of their hating each other. I know Gaia's pissed at me already for some reason—but what is she going to say when she finds out that I played tongue twister with her mortal enemy?

She'll probably shut me out again. And that's what really worries me. Because then who will she have left? No one. She'll be alone. And I can't let that happen. Not to Gaia. I've seen where that leads.

Ella might
have
deliberately
dragged him
up here—
leading **sordid**
business
him on the
proverbial
wild-goose
chase.

"GAIA!" ELLA'S SHRILL VOICE RANG

up the stairs. It seemed she was trying to pack as much disdain as
possible into saying Gaia's name.
As if the mere act of forming that
word was making her physically ill.
"There's somebody here to see you."

Beyond Guilt

The front door slammed.

Gaia's face twisted into a grimace as she pulled a
moth-bitten sweater over her T-shirt. There was only
one person who would possibly show up uninvited at
her house on a Monday morning. He'd done it
before. And right now she was *not* in the mood to
deal with him.

Unless . . .

Could it be Sam?

She swallowed, stealing a quick peek at herself in
the mirror on her closet door. No, it wasn't Sam.
And that was a good thing, too. Her shoulders
sagged. Her hair was in complete disarray—not that
this was a surprise. Her clothes were rumpled and
mismatched. In her fatigues and combat boots she
almost looked like a refugee from some war-torn,
third-world country.

No wonder everybody wanted to hang out with
Heather Gannis. *She* knew how to dress. Hell, yeah.
Throw in some *Vogue*, mix in a little MTV: presto!
That was fashion.

Gaia's fashion only seemed to reflect her sour disposition.

But who cared how she looked?

With a groan she slung her backpack over her shoulder and trotted down the stairwell to the front hall.

Yup. She'd been right all along. Heather Gannis's new best friend smiled at Gaia from his wheelchair as she descended the last flight of steps.

"Hey, G."

"What are you doing here, Ed?" she asked wearily, heading straight for the kitchen. She swung her book bag off her shoulder. It dropped to the front hall floor with a loud *thwack*. *Shouldn't you be having lox and bagels with Heather right now?* she added to herself, feeling petty and sullen.

Ed rolled after her. "I . . . uh, came to freeload breakfast cereals off you. You know, the way I've been doing for the past four months—"

"Where did Ella go?" Gaia interrupted. She reached into a cabinet and yanked a box of Froot Loops off the shelf, then slammed the door so hard that the plates rattled. "You know, she doesn't like it when people just show up unannounced."

"Yeah . . . I got that impression," Ed said. He hesitated in the kitchen doorway. "She just gave me this look and took off." He laughed. "I kind of get the feeling she wants to make this house wheelchair inaccessible."

Great. Now he was going for the wheelchair jokes. Playing the pity card. Enough was enough. Gaia whirled and slammed the box of cereal down on the kitchen table. "What do you *want*, Ed?" she growled.

His expression didn't falter. "Well, for starters, I want to know why you're acting like such a bitch right now," he answered with the same easygoing smile. "We can take it from there."

"I . . ." She couldn't answer. A sense of self-loathing swept over her, smothering her like a black shroud. She lowered her eyes, then glanced out the kitchen window at the charcoal-colored sky. *I'm acting like a bitch because I'm a petty, jealous jerk. I'm acting like a bitch because I can't stand to share you with anyone else. Especially you know who.* But there was no way she could say any of that.

"Look, I'm just a little worn out, all right?" she lied, grabbing a bowl and spoon from the unemptied dishwasher. "I stayed up all night trying to finish *The Great Gatsby*. I didn't even start the paper."

Ed pulled up to the table. "Well, if it's any consolation, neither did I," he said. "That's part of the reason I'm here, actually. I was hoping to do a little early morning plagiarizing."

Gaia met his gaze. "What's *your* excuse?" she asked harshly. "Busy weekend?"

Ed blinked. "What are you talking about?"

"You tell me," she shot back. "I know you spent the

night at Heather's on Friday." *Jesus.* Who *was* she right now? Hearing herself made her sick. She sounded like an out-of-control second grader, throwing a temper tantrum.

Ed's eyes narrowed in seeming disbelief. "Who told you *that?*"

"Your parents," Gaia muttered. She tore open the box of Froot Loops and started pouring them into the bowl.

"Oh, Jesus," Ed moaned. He pushed himself away from the table and shook his head. "For your information, Gaia, I was at the hospital. I just told my parents I was at Heather's so they wouldn't freak out. They had enough on their minds this weekend without dealing with any of *my* shit."

Gaia's head jerked up. She nearly dropped the cereal box. The sick feeling inside her began to grow. "You were at the *hospital?*" she whispered.

He nodded, staring down at his lap. "Yeah. Heather's sister Phoebe . . . Look, it doesn't even matter. That's not the point."

The blood drained from Gaia's face. She put the cereal box down on the table. Her hand was trembling. Heather really *had* been having a crisis. But in Gaia's state of utter self-absorption, she hadn't even considered it. She hadn't even believed it. She'd only focused on how the situation affected *her.*

"The point is," Ed continued, "you're pissed off at me, and I want to know why."

Suddenly Gaia was overcome with an uncontrollable urge to bolt. Immediately. She couldn't sit here anymore. Besides, her appetite was shot. If she answered Ed's question . . . no. That wasn't an option. She'd had enough self-examination for one day. No way was she going to admit to Ed that she was jealous of Heather. She would never show that kind of weakness. To *anyone*.

"I gotta go," Gaia muttered. She stood abruptly and brushed past Ed, without even bothering to close the cereal box or put away her dishes. She snatched her book bag up from the floor of the front hall and grabbed her coat.

"Wait, Gaia!" Ed called after her. "There's something I want to tell you—"

Gaia slammed the front door behind her. She was sure she didn't want to hear what he had to tell her, anyway.

What had happened to the new, open Gaia, ready to deal like a true friend? she wondered miserably as she sped along the sidewalk, away from him.

WHATEVER ELLA NIVEN MIGHT BE, she was *not* an up-and-coming freelance photographer.

Tom was almost certain of that now.

Classic Smoke Screen

He'd been trailing her since Saturday night, stopping only to doze for a few hours here and there—and every action she took seemed to indicate that she was leading another life. A secret life. One carefully hidden from George and the rest of the world.

The most obvious scraps of evidence, of course, were those clandestine trips to that apartment building on the Upper West Side. Judging from the frequency of the visits (four in two days), their brevity (never more than fifteen minutes at a time), and the circuitous routes she took in getting there (never the same route twice), he could deduce that she was reporting to somebody. A superior. Perhaps the person with whom she spoke so frequently on her cell phone.

But whom was she working for? And why?

There were several possible answers, of course. One was that she was working for the agency itself. She might have been assigned to keep an eye on George. That wouldn't surprise him at all, in fact. Spouses were hired to spy on each other all the time. It was an extremely effective way of maintaining security. Unfortunately, the spying often ended up destroying otherwise happy marriages. But then, happy marriages had never been the agency's top priority.

It meant nothing that Tom had never seen Ella's

name on any agency list. He knew very well that no agency member could name *all* of the agency's employees—just as no agency member could detail an entire operation or provide a list of all its activities. The less people knew, the better. And the powers that be would definitely want to keep Ella's employment secret from him. After all, he was George's best friend. He might compromise her status.

Even now, as Tom followed Ella through the gray, wintry streets of the Village to a camera store on Seventh Avenue, he was positive that this errand was simply part of an elaborate act. He hurried past the store window, eyes forward, using his peripheral vision to soak up the scene inside. She was chatting happily with the store clerk about a lens. He almost smiled. This kind of activity was a textbook precaution if one had gone deep cover. A classic smoke screen. Tom could quote the manual word for word: *"Cover professions should consume most of a standard business day. . . . Establish relationships with appropriate merchants and associates. . . . Always assume you have a shadow. . . ."*

He rounded the corner and paused outside a bookstore.

A bitter wind swept down the street. He shivered, pondering his next course of action. No doubt she would spend the rest of the morning being a photographer. Correction: *pretending* to be a photographer.

Maybe he should move on to the surveillance of Sam Moon.

Or maybe he should find out who lived in that apartment building.

He anxiously tapped his foot on the frozen sidewalk. Even as this thought crossed his mind for the thousandth time, he thrust it aside. If he snooped too much and she *was* working for the agency, then he would most likely be discovered. And then he would lose his job—and a short time later, his life. He only needed to consider how his behavior would look to them. Here he was, unwittingly spying on the agency for his own purposes when he should have been working for them overseas. He'd already gone AWOL, for all intents and purposes. Renegade. They didn't need another excuse to terminate him.

On the other hand, there was a distinct possibility that she was working for an enemy. A foreign power, perhaps. Another intelligence community. A crime syndicate. The possibilities were as endless as they were terrifying. And in that case, the agency would *want* to know who lived in that building. Just as much as he did.

But I can't afford to take that risk. Not when I have to make sure I stay alive. Not when Gaia's in so much danger . . .

There was one last possibility, too. One that filled him with dread.

Ella could be working for Loki.

He swallowed, glancing back down the street toward Seventh Avenue. He knew from the agency's database that Loki was in close contact with a "BFF" and an "ELJ." Every time this suspicion crept into the back of Tom's consciousness, he was nearly overwhelmed by an intense desire to find George, to tell him. But he couldn't. Given his friend's current fragile state, even a seed of doubt would tear George apart. No, Tom had to be absolutely sure of Ella's guilt. And there was only one way to do that.

Keep watching.

WHAT WAS THE POINT OF SCHOOL,
anyway?

Gaia took one look around the grim rows of identical lockers and knew instantly that coming here

Mindless Teenage Drones

had been a monumental mistake. She hadn't done her homework. She hated the stinking cafeteria food. (Not nearly enough sugar.) She definitely didn't want to *socialize*.

Not with these mindless teenage drones, churned straight from the pages of *Seventeen* magazine. No, in fact, she wanted to stay as far as possible from two specific members of the student body, those being one Ed Fargo and one Heather Gannis.

So why stay? What did she need with this place?

She couldn't think of one good reason to stay. Not one. This place was a freaking dump. It wasn't as if she needed a formal education. She'd probably read more books by the age of twelve than most of the underpaid English teachers here had read in their entire lifetimes. She had a good grasp of calculus. She sure as hell didn't need to go to gym—not with her freakish build. So what did that leave? Art? Fine. She'd take up finger painting in her spare time. Anyway, her lifelong dream was to be a waitress, and it didn't take a high school diploma to serve two eggs over easy or to get her butt pinched.

Fine. It was a relief. She was glad she'd made *that* decision. School and Gaia Moore would no longer have anything to do with each other.

She turned and shoved her way back to the exit, nearly knocking over a couple of faceless meatheads on her way.

"Watch it, bitch!" one of them snapped.

"Bye!" she called sweetly.

A blast of winter air hit her as she burst out onto the front steps. It was crisp and invigorating. She laughed out loud. A couple of stragglers stared at her: the chronically late, dope-smoking crowd. She blew them a kiss. She was free! Free at last!

It was so easy. So perfectly simple.

The city seemed to stretch out before her, `filled with limitless possibility`. She had the whole day to spend exactly as she pleased. Talk about liberating. She couldn't believe it had taken her *this* long to drop out of school. What had she been thinking, anyway?

Maybe she should just toss her book bag in a garbage can to make it official. It was weighing her down. Nah . . . she might need it for other things. Like to carry around all the money she would win from hustling chess games in the park. Yes. *That's* what she'd do with her time. She'd spend the next few months earning a small fortune on the tables in Washington Square Park (maybe kicking the ass of a random thug or two every now and then, just to keep the area safe)—then she'd blow this town for good. No more Ella and George. No more Ed and Heather. No more creepy uncle. No more Sam—

She stopped short.

Sam.

A twinge of electricity shot down her spine.

He *still* hadn't explained himself. And he still wasn't answering his damn phone, either.

Gaia was riding high on recklessness. Who cared what happened tomorrow? All that mattered was living large this minute. *Now* was the time to confront Sam Moon. She was sick of waiting around and wondering. Fed up. She would go straight to his dorm. If her uncle jumped out at her again, she would ignore him. If Sam was in class, she would just hang around his suite until he got back.

There was no stopping her. Not this time.

" . . . MR. MOON? DID YOU HEAR ME?"

Decomposing Mold

Sam jerked up from his microscope with a start. Dr. Witchell was glaring at him over the rims of his wire-frame glasses.

"We were talking about the rate of decomposition," Dr. Witchell stated.

The words floated over Sam's head. He swallowed. He had no idea what his professor was talking about. And the truly frightening thing was that he'd been sitting in this biochemistry lab for almost half an hour, going through the motions of examining this chunk of decomposing mold—even jotting observations down in a notebook. But his body had been working independently of his brain.

When he looked through the lens, he didn't see thousands of little cells. He saw Ella's wicked smile. He saw Gaia lying unconscious on her front stoop.

"I'm sorry," he finally choked out.

Dr. Witchell sneered. "Sorry?"

"Listen . . . I—I have to go," he stammered. He scrambled to gather his notebook and pencil, then pushed himself away from the table. His stool screeched loudly on the tile floor. A few people around him winced. "I'm sorry—"

"What do you think you're *doing?*" Dr. Witchell demanded, aghast. "You can't just come and go as you please. . . ."

Sam was already sprinting down the hall. Somewhere in the back of his mind, he knew that this was inexcusable. He very well might be jeopardizing his entire college career by running out of class. But he also knew there wasn't any logical reason to stick around anymore. He couldn't concentrate. It wasn't as if he could improve his slipping grades by *pretending* to be studious.

He skidded to a stop by a drinking fountain and ran his face through the lukewarm stream of water. But nothing could calm him down. Every time he thought of Ella, every time he thought of the way she'd just laughed him off Saturday—as if he weren't even *real,* as if he were some kind of *toy*—a wave of panic overtook him. This was no way to live. He knew that. It couldn't even be called *living,* really. Running around the West Village,

hiding in his room, avoiding phone calls, not sleeping . . .
He was going slowly insane. And it scared him.

His eyes darted to the stairwell. He had to get out
of this building. He had to do *something*. He still hadn't
talked to Gaia since Friday. Of course, he knew now
that telling her the truth would solve nothing . . . but
he had to see her face. To say something. Anything. He
still hadn't talked to Heather, either. As far as Heather
was concerned, everything between them was just the
same. He laughed. How crazy was *that*? If she even
knew the tiniest fraction of the truth . . . Of course, he
hadn't heard from her this weekend, which was a little
strange—but maybe *she* was waiting for *him* to call.
That was exactly the kind of game she liked to play.

He had to go see Gaia now. Nothing else mattered. The fact that he might well see Heather in the
process was just another of the sick coincidences in
his life.

ELLA'S STOMACH DROPPED AS THE

Bullet to the Brain

elevator whisked her up to
Loki's apartment, and it wasn't
simply due to the speed of the
ascent. For the past forty-
eight hours his behavior had

been disarmingly . . . *calm*. Friendly. Affectionate, even. As if her lies and her failure had been abruptly forgotten or forgiven—both of which were impossible. No, she knew that he had a new strategy, a new agenda.

Her knees wobbled as the doors slid silently open. Every time she'd been here this weekend, she'd half expected a bullet to enter her brain the moment she stepped into the hallway. But once again she was greeted only with silence. She stepped quickly across the plush carpeting and rapped on Loki's door.

"Come in," came the muffled reply. "It's open."

Ella turned the knob and stepped inside, hesitating in the foyer. Loki was lounging on the lone couch in the living room, flipping through a *New Yorker*. She frowned, not knowing what to make of the scene. It was so oddly domestic. She didn't think she'd ever seen him read anything other than intelligence reports or financial statements.

He flashed her a relaxed smile. "Anything new to report?"

She bit her lip, debating again whether or not to tell him about Saturday's incident with George. It was probably best just to get it out in the open. Loki invariably discovered the truth, anyway.

"George thinks I'm having an affair," she whispered.

Loki snickered. "That's something he and I have in common."

"But it's not *true!*" she cried. "I'm not—"

"Shhh," he murmured. "There's no need to get excited."

She held her breath, staring at him. He sighed and tossed the magazine on the barren floor, then stood up. His shirt was halfway unbuttoned and untucked. The smooth muscles of his chest were plainly visible beneath the flimsy fabric. Ella's breath came a little faster. Even in her fearful state, she couldn't help but desire him; she couldn't help but drink in his rugged sexiness. He wasn't a man, Loki. He was a *force*. She lowered her eyes.

"So you're not having an affair," Loki stated. "Fine. I believe you. The question is, how are you going to make George believe you?"

Ella shrugged. "I—I . . . don't know," she stammered. "I told him that my career was taking up a lot of time. I told him things would get better when I wasn't as busy."

Loki laughed quietly. "Spoken like a true housewife. The nervousness and evasion is perfect. You never cease to amaze me, Ella. Your skills are exquisite."

The words sent a shudder down her spine. *Too bad I really am nervous and evasive,* she thought, not trusting herself to lift her gaze. Why did she always feel so helpless around him? So out of control?

Again she perversely wished that he could see her with Sam or George—even if only for an instant—so that he could witness for himself just how *in* control she was when it came to the rest of her life. Then he would know for certain that she was worthy of his love.

"And what of Gaia?" he asked.

"She's in school," Ella muttered. "It's a Monday. That crippled boy came by to pick her up."

"Right, right," Loki mused. "Ed. He's harmless enough."

Something's definitely going on, she thought with a chill. Loki never dismissed anything so casually when it came to Gaia's life. He dissected every little event in a thousand different ways, searching for any possible significance. So his reaction must have been false. His whole demeanor was false.

But what was real?

"Well, I think that's enough business for today," Loki stated suddenly.

His voice was thick, husky. He stepped briskly across the room and grabbed her chin, lifting her head so that her eyes were less than three inches from his own. His breath came in quick, short gasps. Before she could even cry out, he smothered her lips in a harsh kiss. She found herself kissing him back . . . slowly at first, then with greater passion and finally abandon.

There was no resisting Loki. There was only succumbing to his will.

NO WAY.

The Color of Chalk

Heather shook her head, blinking. Obviously her imagination was running just a bit wild. Obviously she was just paranoid. No way could that disheveled, crazy-looking person lurking in the hall be *Sam*.

Her eyes darted to the clock, then to Mr. Hirschberg (still rambling on about Daisy Buchanan), then back to the little window in the classroom door. Class was almost over. Maybe she was just—

Jesus. She flinched. The face filled the window for an instant, then vanished again. It *was* Sam. Either that or his evil twin. What the hell was he doing here? And why did he look so terrible? Her heart started to pound. This wasn't good. Something was definitely wrong. He was drenched in sweat: wide-eyed, pale. His curly, ginger-colored hair was unkempt. He looked like he hadn't bathed in a week. At least, not from the neck up.

Ed must have called him.

Oh God. There was no other reason he'd come hunt her down in the middle of a school day, looking like a psycho. She squirmed in her seat. She could just picture the conversation. A man-to-man kind of thing. Her insides clenched. Sometimes Ed could be a real idiot. And it was just the kind of macho stunt he'd pull—out of a misguided sense of decency. *"Look, pal, I just thought you had a right to know. Heather and I are back together again, all right? So stay—*

The bell shattered her thoughts.

She stole another quick peek at the window. Shit. Sam was staring straight at her. A bunch of kids jostled her as they gathered their bags and scurried for the door, but she couldn't move. She felt like her butt was glued to the seat.

"Miss Gannis?" Mr. Hirschberg asked. The class was quickly emptying. "Is everything all right?"

"Uh . . . yeah," she croaked. She forced herself to stand. Her legs were shaky. She should have called Sam herself. She should have done it the second she'd gotten home last night. This was *not* the way he was supposed to find out. But truthfully, Sam hadn't even entered her mind. All she could think of was Ed. Even this morning she was still reeling from the ecstasy of that kiss. . . .

She stepped into the hall.

"Heather," Sam gasped.

She swallowed, unable to look him in the eye. Instead she stared down at the sea of moving legs and feet. "What, uh . . . what are you doing here?" she murmured. "Shouldn't you be in the lab right now?"

"I can't concentrate," he said. His voice was clipped. "I really need to—I came here because—Look, never mind."

His eyes were darting wildly up and down the hallway. He moved away from her. His stare was glazed and preoccupied. Suddenly he seemed to have forgotten she was there. "I gotta go," he mumbled.

Heather's eyes narrowed. "Why *are* you here?" she asked. "What's going on? Maybe we should talk."

He hardly seemed to hear her. "Yeah, well, maybe some other time. . . ." He shot a manic glance at the kids rushing past them, then ran a hand through his damp hair. "Look, I can't explain it all right now, okay? It's just . . . things are a little crazy right now."

Translation: You're *a little crazy right now,* Heather thought, taking a step back. She was starting to get freaked out. It seemed less and less likely that this little surprise visit had anything to do with her and Ed. No, clearly there was something else, and she had a strong suspicion it had to do with Gaia. And the sad thing was, Heather really didn't care at this point. Not after what she'd shared with Ed. She just wanted to get away from Sam. As fast as possible. God, did he look like crap. His skin was the color of chalk.

"You're looking for Gaia," Heather stated flatly.

Sam didn't bother to deny it. "You don't know where she is, do you?" he persisted, obviously desperate.

"Try the local satanic cult," Heather muttered. She turned and hurried down the hall. Her next class was in the opposite direction, but she'd just have to be a little late.

As she broke into a jog and rounded the corner, she realized for certain what she'd suspected over the past few weeks: She and Sam were over. For good.

IT WASN'T UNTIL THE STAIRWELL

door had slammed shut behind her that Gaia started breathing again. Not that she had to worry. She didn't even have to sneak past the security guard this time. His face was buried in a *Sports Illustrated*. She could have walked right past him with a submachine gun. That would be kind of funny, actually. Maybe he assumed that nobody would try to break into the dormitory during the middle of the day. Whatever.

A familiar haze of conflicting emotions enveloped

Unsent Messages

her as she climbed the stairs to the fourth floor. She wasn't scared. But she did feel that electric fizz in her veins. She couldn't tell if she was more upset about the possibility of Sam's being there or the possibility of his *not* being there. Of course, chances were good that he was in class. It was just before noon on a Monday. Prime class hours. She should know. Conversely, chances were slim that he was in his room having sex with Heather—but then, Gaia couldn't be *too* sure. Judging from her past surprise visits, that seemed to be a fairly common occurrence.

Her breath quickened as she walked down the hall to his suite. The door was closed. Maybe nobody was home. She knocked once, but there was no answer. Then again. Nobody was home. On a whim, she gave the doorknob a try.

It turned.

Gaia frowned. Weren't these guys worried about theft? This was New York City, for God's sake. Did they actually have faith in that moron downstairs? Oh, well. She stepped through the pile of empty pizza boxes strewn about the little common room (what was it about college that turned otherwise intelligent males into pigs, anyway?), then put her ear to Sam's door.

Nothing.

She turned that knob, too. Though no longer broken, it was also, thankfully, unlocked.

Okay. Her heart was now officially racing. Her mind, of course, was simultaneously numb and alert. She'd done it. She'd come to confront Sam Moon. On his turf. This was where he lived. This was where he slept. In this little cell, no bigger than a closet. She'd been here before. The tiny room held awful memories, but a few foggy (possibly fantasized) ecstatic ones as well.

So what did she do now?

Wait, she supposed. She collapsed onto Sam's unmade bed. The curtains were still drawn, but a lone shaft of light illuminated the dust motes in the air. She breathed the faint smell of him left on his sheets and felt an almost chemical longing for him seep through her body.

There were footsteps in the hall.

She stiffened and peered out into the common room, hoping to catch sight of him breezing through the entranceway. Nope. It was some buffed fraternity type in a sweatshirt who looked like he'd been taking steroids since the age of three. She sighed. The glowing red numbers on Sam's digital clock changed from 11:59 to 12:00. Maybe he'd come back here for lunch.

With her luck, probably not, though.

Her eyes fell to a photo on top of his desk. A photo of a little boy . . . she squinted at it. *Hold on.* A puzzled smile spread across her face. Was that Sam? It must be:

The boy had the same brownish red hair, the same hazel eyes. He was holding a trophy. Of course. A chess trophy. For some reason, the picture brought a lump to Gaia's throat. He looked so happy, framed by his parents—but a little lost, too. Even as a little child, Sam had a melancholy aura, as if his smile was really concealing something deeper and more complicated—

The phone rang.

Shit. Gaia dropped the photo. It fell with a dull thud onto the bed. She glanced into the common room again. Obviously she shouldn't answer that. But maybe it was Sam, calling in to check his messages. In that case, she could intercept him and let him know that she was here, that she was waiting for him. Without thinking, she lunged for the receiver—bumping his chair, which slammed into his desk. *Whoops.* A person could hardly move in here.

"Hello?" she panted.

There was a click.

"Hello? Hello?"

No answer. The line was dead.

Gaia pursed her lips. She dropped the phone on the hook.

Then she noticed something. By bumping Sam's desk, she'd knocked his computer out of sleep mode. And there, on the screen, was an open file labeled Unsent Messages.

Her breath stopped short. Her eyes flashed down the list.

Oh my God.

Every single unsent message was addressed to her.

SHE WASN'T IN SCHOOL.

After searching the entire building, scouring every god-damn classroom—not to mention the gym, the cafeteria,

Faking It

and the computer center—he'd finally come to the inevitable conclusion: Gaia wasn't here. Even worse, nobody seemed to know *where* she was. Not Heather. Not Ed. Not even members of the faculty. This was just perfect. On the one day he'd decided to track her down at *school*, where she was pretty much required by law to be, she'd ditched.

He stood just inside the front doors, shaking his head. He didn't exactly relish the thought of going back outside into the freezing cold.

Gaia could be sick, of course. But somehow the thought of Gaia's being bedridden with the flu just didn't seem plausible. Gaia was too *strong* to get sick. On the other hand, she might be faking it.

Maybe she'd decided to feign an illness so she could stay in bed all day. *That* wasn't so far-fetched. Sam wanted to do the exact same thing himself.

He flung open the door and flew down the steps of the school building, searching the block for a pay phone. *There.* On the corner. He dashed across the street, fumbling for a quarter as he dodged a couple of cars and a bike messenger. Horns blared; he didn't notice. He snatched up the phone, dropped the coin into the slot, and punched in her number.

After two rings somebody picked up.

"Niven residence."

It was her foster father. Sam hesitated for a moment. "Um, yes, hello," he said nervously. "I was just wondering . . . is Gaia there, please?"

"No, she's at school." His voice took on a harsher edge. "Who is this?"

"It's . . . a friend," he replied lamely. Panicking, he hung up the phone. Gaia was at large. As far as he knew, she wasn't the type to skip school. So maybe she had a good reason. Maybe she was very upset.

Maybe Ella had upset her.

He took a deep breath of frozen air. There was nothing more he could do. It was out of his hands. He should just go home.

GAIA WAS NOT A SNOOP. SHE *HATED*
snoops. Her father (may he
rot in hell) had made a living
out of snooping. He'd devoted
his whole miserable life to
invading privacy and tearing
people's lives apart. The very
thought of following in his

You're a Hypocrite

footsteps made Gaia's stomach turn. Not only was
going through somebody's private e-mail unethical,
immoral, and *slimy*—it was against the law. Or at
least she thought it was.

On the other hand, Gaia had never given much
thought to the law. The only rules that had ever
applied were her own. She lived her life by her own
code of honor. It was inviolate, unbreakable.

You're a hypocrite. And you know it.

Her gaze roved over the computer screen. She
couldn't stop staring at the list. It was so *long*. There
must be at least ten messages. And they were all
addressed to gaia13@alloymail.com. They *were*
intended for her eyes. Well, they had been at one
point. Right. So in a way, she wasn't snooping. She was
simply catching up on what should have been hers in
the first place.

You're a hypocrite. And you know it.

She wished she could shut up that stupid
voice in her head. Everybody rationalized

something every once in a while, didn't they?

Clenching her jaw, she grabbed the mouse and clicked on the first message.

From: smoon@alloymail.com
To: gaia13@alloymail.com
Time: 5:32 P.M.
Re: Why I took off

Gaia,

You're probably wondering what happened to me and why I just dumped you on your stoop like that. I never would have left you alone

<<UNSENT>>

Okay. This wasn't so bad. She relaxed a little. Sam wasn't confessing any deep, dark secrets. There were no major revelations here. And while he wasn't exactly apologizing, he did feel the need to explain himself. That was something. A start. His heart was in the right place—or at least heading there.

She clicked the next message.

From: smoon@alloymail.com
To: gaia13@alloymail.com
Time: 5:33 P.M.
Re: Why I took off

```
Gaia,
    I'm sorry about what happened Friday night. But
there's something you have to know. It involves
                    <<UNSENT>>
```

Hmmm. He was holding back. She could see that a
pattern was forming. These were the beginnings of
abandoned thoughts. Fragments. She could definitely
relate. She had her *own* stash of unsent mail to
Sam sitting in her hard drive.

That's why you're a hypocrite.

Screw it. She shook her head and scrolled
forward.

VISIT NUMBER FIVE. IN FORTY-EIGHT

hours. Only this one
was lasting a lot longer
than usual.

A Target for the Plucking

Tom eyed the apart-
ment entrance from his
convenient perch in the
coffee shop window. Ella
had disappeared under the awning nearly an hour
ago. She seemed to have developed a rapport with the
doorman as well.

The longer she stayed inside, the more certain he became that she was *not* an operative for the agency.

He knew for a fact that the agency wouldn't tolerate such a lax attitude. Her job as a photographer seemed to end sometime in the midmorning. Very poor form. As soon as she'd departed the camera store, she'd headed straight for the subway and proceeded directly uptown on the number-nine train. She didn't even make an *attempt* at losing a potential shadow.

Now that he thought about it, *no* government would tolerate such indiscretion.

That left terrorists. Criminals.

Loki.

A muffled beep rang inside his coat pocket. Tom felt a brief twitter of nervousness. This very well could be the agency, calling to check up on him, to demand why he hadn't been doing his job. He pulled out his cell phone and flipped it open.

"Yes?"

"Gaia's disappeared."

George. Tom's heart lurched in his chest. "Are you sure?" he whispered.

"Some boy just called looking for her," George answered briskly. "I called the school, and they said she was absent."

Tom clutched the phone, fighting back panic. "Okay," he said. "She doesn't usually skip school, does she?"

"To be honest, I have no idea. Like I said before, you trained her well."

"It could be nothing," Tom said, mostly to himself. "All teenagers pull these kinds of stunts at some time or another. And if things aren't great at home . . ." He stopped. He shouldn't have said that last part, but he couldn't help it. Besides, it was the truth. Things *were* bad at home. His thoughts raced. He was having a hard time breathing.

"I just thought you should know," George remarked. If he was offended, he let it slide. "I'm sorry."

"No . . . thank you." Tom swallowed.

"I'll keep you posted," George said.

Tom snapped the cell phone shut, staring at the apartment entrance. Suddenly a thought occurred to him. Ella might have known that he was trailing her all along. She might have deliberately dragged him up here—leading him on the proverbial wild-goose chase. And all the while he'd left Gaia vulnerable: a target for the plucking.

Loki's target.

To: gaia13@alloymail.com

Surrender

Time: 5:34 P.M.
Re: Why I took off
Gaia,

I've done something terrible. I know this is
no excuse, but I had no idea she was

<<UNSENT>>

If Gaia had been able to feel fear, *this* message
definitely would have frightened her. That's because
Sam was clearly afraid. His tone had shifted. He was
no longer abject; he was rushed, desperate.
What was he scared of, though? And what terrible
thing could he have possibly done? But the
most troubling part was that one little three-letter
word: *she*.

Gaia leaned back in his swivel chair.

She glanced out into the empty common room
again. Maybe she'd seen enough. Maybe she should
just get the hell out of here. She wasn't solving any
mysteries; she was just uncovering new ones.
This stupid exercise merely proved what she'd
known all along: that snooping never resulted in
anything positive. She didn't have to look any further than her own screwed-up family to remember
that.

The computer hummed for a second.

All of a sudden, a 3-D envelope cascaded to the forefront of the screen.

"You have e-mail," a computerized voice announced.

Gaia tensed. *"You"* doesn't mean *"me,"* she furiously reminded herself. *It means Sam.* Still, she was right here . . . and she'd already answered his phone. She'd already broken into his room. Her "code" was clearly a thing of the past—at least when it came to Sam. She'd thrown her scruples out the window. That was no justification, though. It wasn't even an excuse. It was simply a surrender.

She couldn't help herself. Her hand was already darting toward the mouse, like a snake going after its prey. She double clicked the icon, fighting to ignore the shame and self-loathing that threatened to stop her. The envelope unfolded.

Her eyes flicked to the top of the letter. To: smoon. From: ELJ

Darling . . .

Heather, Gaia thought dismally.

It had to be. In spite of the random initials, it had to be Heather. Gaia had no idea that Heather could be so corny, though. She almost felt like printing this thing out and showing it to Ed. If he saw *this,* he probably wouldn't be so eager to pal around with Heather so much.

*I don't have much time. If the owner of this com-
puter knew what I was doing . . . I know you're
trying to avoid me, but if you look deep within your
soul, you'll see that you can't deny your attraction
to me.*

Gaia snickered. Christ. This wasn't corny; it was
pitiful. Heather should consider a career as a teen
romance novelist. Reading this thing was like watching
some horrible accident. Gaia was revolted, but she
couldn't turn her eyes away.

*Forgive me for the way I acted on the street on
Saturday. I'm under so much stress. But I must see you
again. Name the time and place. I'll be there.*

Gaia's eyes reached the sign-off.

At first the name didn't seem to register. It was as if
some mechanism in her brain had shut down; she
couldn't process the visual information. There was no
way that *this* name could be *here*. It was simply impossible. Some glitch in the server. A malfunction. Gaia
blinked. She rubbed her eyes.

But the name didn't disappear, or shift, or morph
into Heather's name. It remained there on the screen.
Mocking her. Tearing what little remained of her
self-esteem to shreds.

She began to hyperventilate.

She was practically *gagging*.

But at least she was skipping right over the denial
stage this time. Right over it. Straight into anger. Into

fury. Because at that moment the pieces of a terrible puzzle she hadn't even known existed began to slide into place. Sam's behavior now made perfect sense. And the world was that much crueler for it.

Love, Ella

THE GIRL SPRINTING OUT OF HIS

dorm was not Gaia. That girl—the one in the cargo pants and wool hat and overcoat, the one running in the opposite direction down Eleventh Street . . . she was not Gaia. She just *looked* like Gaia.

This had happened to Sam once before. At a party. He'd been drunk. Actually, that was putting it mildly. He'd been plastered. And pissed off. And his thoughts had been so *focused* on Gaia, so *intent* on her, that when he'd seen a wild mane of long blond hair, he'd just naturally assumed . . .

A Million Complex Chemical Reactions

Obviously the same thing was happening to him now.

As a biochemistry major, he knew that the brain could play tricks on a person. A million complex chemical and electrical reactions went into forming one simple thought. So if the synapses had been saturated with alcohol, or deprived of sleep, or subject to undue stress . . . well, then, a million things could potentially go wrong.

Because there was no way that person was Gaia. None at all.

He was too tired to chase her, anyway.

She grows more beautiful with each passing day.

Sitting across from her in that frozen park was the closest I've come to magic in a long while. I was a little boy again. The horrors that have consumed me for so long suddenly ceased to exist. For that brief period, I was completely entranced. *She* had power over *me*. It was intoxicating. And terrifying.

She truly *is* more dangerous than I'd suspected.

And so much like Katia. So much like my love.

I hadn't noticed the resemblance before. I was only able to see my face in her own. And Tom's, too, of course. But Katia is there as well: in the curve of her cheek, in her smooth, ruby lips. In her strength.

I lost you, Katia—but you and I were never meant to be. *This* is my destiny. I've sacrificed everything for it. I've worn a hundred faces, more than any man

should wear in a lifetime. But
soon I'll only have to wear one.

Soon my life will change. Soon
I'll rid myself of all the foul
sycophants who use me for their
own purposes.

Soon Gaia and I will be
together. Forever.

here is a
sneak peek of
Fearless™ #11:
TRUST™

Sam and Ella.

Sam Moon: The only guy I've ever desired.

Ella Niven: The evil witch who poses as my guardian.

The two of them . . . together.

A part of me still refuses to believe it. True, I always knew that Ella was twisted. I always knew that behind the designer clothes and stupid facade lurked a schemer who was playing her husband for a chump. I even suspected that she was having an affair. Or something bad. Nobody's *that* vacant.

But never could I have possibly imagined that she was cheating on George with *Sam*.

And you know what the real kicker is? I actually feel sorry for Heather Gannis. I do. After all, Sam is still supposedly going out with Heather. I used to hate her for that. Okay, I hated her for a bunch of other stuff, too. But I remember thinking about Sam and Heather together—no, scratch that— *seeing* Sam and Heather together, in bed . . . actually, forget it. No point in rehashing the past. Even now it turns my stomach. But at least it makes *sense*. At least I can understand it. Sam and Heather are pretty much the same age. They hang out in the same social scene. They're both smart, attractive, whatever . . . blah, blah, blah. People wouldn't give them a second glance, even if they were making out in the middle of Broadway.

On the other hand, somebody would probably look twice at a college kid who was tongue wrestling with a thirty-something bimbo. Especially if said bimbo dresses like a teenage hooker.

I guess the biggest question is this: How the hell did it even *happen*? How did they meet? Where? When? I've been through a thousand scenarios, over and over again, and the only one that seems even remotely plausible is that Sam sought out Ella on purpose. Or vice versa. Either way, it doesn't really matter. What matters is that

it was a deliberate act. Somehow,
for some reason, Sam and Ella got
it into their heads that they had
to humiliate me, that they had to
drive the final nail into the coffin
of my already miserable life.

And they succeeded.

I will say this, though:
sneaking into Sam's room and
reading the e-mail Ella sent him
was strangely liberating. If you
truly have nothing to lose, then
you are truly free—in the most
real sense of the word.

Yes, on one level, they
destroyed me. But they also
opened a new door. They *changed*
me. Because now I don't care
about using my special gifts
(being fearless, expertise in a
variety of martial arts, and
near-perfect marksmanship) just
to kick the asses of scumbags who
prey on the weak and innocent.

No. Now I'm going to use those
gifts for revenge.

And I'm looking forward to it.

OFFICIAL RULES FOR "WIN A HAND-HELD PC AT ALLOY.COM"

NO PURCHASE NECESSARY. Sweepstakes begins June 1, 2000 and ends July 31, 2000. Entrants must be 14 years or older as of June 1, 2000 and a legal U.S. resident to enter. Corporate entities are not eligible. Employees and the immediate family members of such employees (or people living in the same household) of Alloy Online, Inc., Simon & Schuster, Inc., and 17th Street Productions and their respective advertising, promotion, production agencies and the affiliated companies of each are not eligible. Participation in this sweepstakes constitutes contestant's full and unconditional agreement to and acceptance of the Official Sweepstakes Rules.

HOW TO ENTER: To enter, visit the Alloy Web site at www.alloy.com. Submit your entry by fully completing the entry form at the site. Entries must be received by July 31, 2000, 11:59 p.m., Eastern Standard Time. There is no charge or cost to register. No mechanically reproduced entries accepted. One entry per email address. Simon & Schuster, Inc., Alloy Online, Inc., and 17th Street Productions and their respective agents are not responsible for incomplete, lost, late, damaged, illegible, or misdirected email or for technical, hardware or software failures of any kind, lost or unavailable network connections, or failed, incomplete, garbled or delayed computer transmissions which may limit a user's ability to participate in the sweepstakes. All notifications in the sweepstakes will be sent by email. Sponsor is not responsible, and may disqualify you if your email address does not work or if it is changed without prior notice to us via email at contest@alloymail.com. Sponsor reserves the right to cancel or modify the sweepstakes if fraud or technical failures destroy the integrity of the sweepstakes as determined by Sponsor, in its sole discretion. If the sweepstakes is so canceled, announced winner will receive prize to which s/he is entitled as of the date of cancellation.

RANDOM DRAWING: Prize Winner will be selected in a random drawing from among all eligible entries on August 1, 2000 to be conducted by Alloy Online designated judges, whose decisions are final. Winner will be notified by email on or about August 4, 2000. Odds of winning the prize depends on the number of eligible entries received.

PRIZE: (1): A hand-held PC (Approximate retail value: $2,000) Prize is subject to all federal, state and local taxes, which are the sole responsibility of the winner. Prize is not transferable. No cash substitution, transfer or assignment of prize will be allowed, except by Sponsor in which case a prize of equal or greater value will be awarded.

GENERAL: All federal, state and local laws and regulations apply. Void in Puerto Rico and wherever prohibited or restricted by law. By entering, winner or if applicable winner's parent or legal guardian consents to use of winner's name by Sponsor without additional compensation. Entries become Sponsor's property and will not be returned. For a copy of these official rules, send a self-addressed stamped envelope to Alloy 151 West 26th Street, 11th Floor, NY, NY 10001, Attn: Fearless Hand-Held PC.

AFFIDAVIT OF ELIGIBILTY/RELEASE: To be eligible to win, winner will be required to sign and return an affidavit of eligibility/release of liability (except where prohibited by law). Winner under the age of 18 must have their parent or guardian sign the affidavit and release as well. Failure to sign and return the affidavit or release within 14 days, or to comply with any term or condition in these Official Rules may result in disqualification and the prize being awarded to an alternate winner. Return of any prize notification/prize as undeliverable may result in disqualification and the awarding of the prize to an alternate winner. By accepting prize, winner grants Sponsor permission to use his or her name, picture, portrait, likeness and voice for advertising, promotional and/or publicity purposes connected with this sweepstakes without additional compensation (except where prohibited by law).

By entering, entrants agree to be bound by these official rules and the decisions of the Sponsor which are final. Entrants agree that neither Simon & Schuster, Inc. nor Sponsor shall have responsibility or liability for (1) telephone, electronic, network, internet or computer malfunctions, failures or difficulties injury, (2) errors in transmission, (3) any condition caused by events beyond the control of Simon & Schuster, Inc. and the Sponsor which may cause this sweepstakes to be disrupted or corrupted or (4) any injury, loss or damage of any kind arising out of participation in this sweepstakes or the acceptance or use of the prize.

WINNER: The winner's first name and state of residence will be posted at www.alloy.com on August 10, 2000 or, for the winner's name and state of residence available after August 15, 2000, send a self-addressed, stamped, #10 envelope to: Alloy 151 West 26th Street 11th Floor, NY, NY 10001, Attn: Fearless Hand-Held PC.